Millstone City

By S. P. Bailey

© 2012 by S. P. Bailey

ISBN 978-0-9843603-5-2

All rights reserved.
Printed in the U.S.A.

This is a work of fiction. Names, characters, business entities, places, and incidents either are the product of the author's imagination or are used fictitiously. Any resemblance to actual persons, either living or dead, business entities, events, or locales is entirely coincidental.

Published by Zarahemla Books
869 East 2680 North
Provo, UT 84604 U.S.A.
info@zarahemlabooks.com
ZarahemlaBooks.com

"In *Millstone City*, the LDS mission novel and the thriller collide to create something new: an intense, gritty story that is nevertheless shot through with resilience, honesty, optimism, and, yes, that certain willful naïveté that missionaries possess. Call it Mormon neo-noir. Or full-throttle faithful realism. Whatever you dub this hybrid, clearly S. P. Bailey is well versed in both of the literary streams he's working with, and I'm very pleased to see him cross them to such good effect."

—William Morris, founder of the Mormon arts and culture blog *A Motley Vision*

"It isn't often that a thrill ride of a read is as literary as it is escapist, but Bailey's novel meets that mark. *Millstone City* so captivated me that I gave up a night's sleep to read it, cover to cover."

—Lisa Torcasso Downing, author and *Sunstone* fiction editor

"This novel is a great read on several levels. The conflict between holy desires and the unholy world creates much of the story's tension. But the reasons you'll want to read this book include its nonstop acceleration, constant switchbacks, and overall edge-of-your-seatiness. Even while the missionaries' days are filled with threats from armed thugs and desperate attempts to skip town, they continue to perform their work: visiting, seeking, teaching, even sneaking in a lesson to an interrogating police officer. It's a thrilling read and nearly impossible to put down once you start."

—Theric Jepson, coeditor of *Monsters & Mormons*

Chapter One

I PUT ON MY MISSIONARY outfit with the lights off. All except the name tag—white letters on a black plastic rectangle. It says *Elder Carson* above the name of the church. A mosquito circles my head. Its high-pitched buzz goes loud and soft and loud again. It stops. I slap at the tingle on my neck, and I wipe the palm of my hand—a spattering of blood and mosquito parts—on my pants.

It is after midnight when I push open the apartment door. We keep a strict schedule: wake up at six thirty, work from nine thirty to nine thirty, lights out at ten thirty. The door squeals as I pull it shut. Elder Nordgren doesn't stir. I shared a room with my brother growing up, and Nordgren is nothing like him. Nordgren doesn't snore. He never stays up with me for hours talking about sports, movies, and girls. He is a deep sleeper. He has at least three tattoos.

It is a hot night. Humid like always. The scent of the ocean, a mixture of saline freshness and marine decay, fills my lungs. Only the rain ever supplies a break from the sticky air. Faint music plays in a bar down on the beach, a guitar sobbing a gentle, bitter little *samba*. Waves crash on the sand in a rhythm so regular I hardly notice it anymore. Other than that, things are quiet.

The *Opa* is not far from our apartment. Maybe one kilometer. I start walking. I keep to a long narrow avenue parallel to the beach and the main highway, but a few blocks inland. It is gray cobblestone set in coarse white cement. The vast mango trees lining both sides of the street are black and still. Here and there overripe mangos rot on the sidewalk. Their acid-sweet odor burns in my nose.

This is Olinda. Northeastern Brazil. The easternmost point of the Western Hemisphere. The houses I pass are big. They have tall concrete walls topped with razor wire or steel spikes or shards of broken beer bottles, translucent green and brown and blue. A nice neighborhood.

I set off some motion lights. I laugh, quietly, at the thought that the owners of these garish fortresses just off the beach—places generally impenetrable to missionaries working door to door—might think that I'm a prowler. I'm harmless, of course. I was a Boy Scout before my mission: trustworthy, loyal, helpful, friendly, courteous, kind, and so on, right down the list.

The word *opa* means "hi" in Portuguese, and it's also the excessively cute name of the phone company. The little Opa store in the old part of Olinda is open all night. It is a small room with a desk and some phone booths—a holdover from the days before mobile phones. It serves people who have neither a landline nor a mobile, including homesick Mormon missionaries.

I go inside. The walls and low ceiling are chalky white plaster. Every other surface—the desk, the phone booths, the floor—is brilliant blue plastic. I dig around in my backpack for a phone card.

"Elder Carson," the guy at the counter says. He is gaunt. Skeletal even. About sixty. He has a salt-and-pepper beard and sorrowful glassy brown eyes.

I look up, afraid that a member of the church has recognized me. I'm breaking several rules: being alone, being out after midnight, calling people back home not on Christmas or Mother's Day. I usually carry a little white book of mission rules in my left breast pocket. We call it the "white bible." It is back on my dresser with my name tag and a laminated notecard of irregular verb conjugations.

"Juvelino." The guy unfolds a bony brown hand and places it over his heart. "We are friends. You came to my house! You gave me one of your books!"

I remember that Nordgren and I taught this guy a first discussion about a month ago. Juvelino seemed to be bored out of his mind. He said no to almost everything. No, I won't schedule another appointment. No, I won't pray with you. No, I won't visit your church sometime. But he was glad to take a copy of the book.

"Right," I say. "It's been a while. How are you?"

"*Bacana*," Juvelino says. "And you?"

"*Tudo jóia.*"

"*E aí, rapaz?*" Juvelino says. "What can I do for you?"

"International call."

"All right," he says. "Sign in, *meu amigo*." He slides a clipboard and a pen across the blue counter and watches me intently.

I put my name down twice: autograph and print. I step into the first booth, swipe the phone card, and dial her number. There is a long pause. The sound of connections being made over the thousands of miles between Brazil and Utah.

"Hello?" she says.

"Lilly, it's me."

"Who is this?" she says.

"Elder Car—Zach."

"Car-Zach?"

"Zach, Lilly. This is Zach."

"What's wrong?" she says. "Are you all right?"

"I miss you."

"I miss you too," she says.

"How is—everything?"

Silence.

"Did I lose you?" I say. "Hello?"

"Normal," she says. "Zach, time goes by so slowly. You're such a jerk!"

"What?"

"You made me cry," she says. "I keep thinking this is a dream. I miss you—and you are such a jerk."

"I wanted to hear your voice."

"You're breaking the rules," she says.

"It's your fault. I can't stop thinking about you."

"I know how to kiss boys so they don't forget."

"Boys, huh? Plural? You have something you want to tell me?"

"Shut up!" she says. "What about you, Elder? Say hello to all those hot Brazilian chicks for me."

"It's true I guess. My name tag must be some kind of aphrodisiac."

"Maybe you'll get sent home," she says. "Maybe? Please?"

"You'd never marry me if that happened."

"A girl can dream," she says. "Tell me something about your day. What did you do? Where did you go?"

"It was P-day. We toured some old church with, you know, chanting monks and everything. That was cool. We played basketball in Recife with the presidente. We got groceries and did laundry."

"That gives me all kinds of fantasy material," she says. "You playing basketball. You pushing around a grocery cart. Monks on the soundtrack. You do your laundry by hand, right?"

"Washboard and everything. I'd be willing to say I did my laundry without a shirt on today. You know, if it makes for better material."

"Oh bronze Adonis," she says. "Washboards everywhere."

"That's Elder Adonis to you."

"I love you," she says.

"I love you too. I wrote you a letter today."

"That's sweet. I guess I'll see it in three weeks?"

"Something like that. Watch your mailbox for my letter from three weeks ago. I loved you three weeks ago too, so it works."

Silence. I feel like we are both holding our breath.

"You have to go?" she finally says.

"I better get back. It's the middle of the night."

"Where's your companion?"

"Calling his girlfriend. He's in the next booth. You want to say hi to him?"

"Seriously?"

"Dude's asleep. He doesn't even know I'm gone. Trust me. The guy will still be sawing logs when I get back."

"Zach—you are bad."

"Pure evil," I say.

"I'm going to bed soon," she says. "To dream of you."

"I'll dream of you too."

There is another long pause.

"Bye, Lilly."

"Bye, jerk. I'm crying again."

"Stop it."

"Bye."

"I'll call again soon."

"Don't, Zach. It makes it worse."

"I'll call again tomorrow."

"Evil," she says. "This is where I encourage you to focus on the work."

"Nice try," I say.

"Bye."

"Good night."

I hang up. I sit there for a minute grinning to myself. I stand. "You got a restroom?" I say to Juvelino.

Juvelino points to a glossy blue door in the back.

I'm in there, washing my hands, when I hear a vehicle pull up. It sounds big, a truck or a hot rod. That's unusual in the land of compact Fiats and Hyundais and Volkswagens. Doors slam, but the engine keeps idling, a low grumble. The front door of the Opa opens and shuts. A man says something sharp. I can't make it out.

"Please," Juvelino cries. "No."

I open the bathroom door just a crack. There are two men in front of the desk. They have guns on Juvelino. One of them is slight, maybe five six and a hundred forty pounds. He wears black slacks, patent leather shoes, and a white shirt, unbuttoned and wide open at the neck. The tattoo on his chest is a jagged green splotch. A Martian birthmark. "*Filho de puta*," he says.

The other one is bigger. He wears shorts, flip-flops, and an oversized T-shirt. He looks over his shoulder, and his eyes meet mine. *He looks like Heitor,* I think. It is Heitor. I baptized him two months ago. It has only been maybe four hours since I saw him with his family at a little party. He is scared in a way I have never seen him. He gives me a look that is desperate and menacing and sorry. He gestures for me to get back in the bathroom.

I step back, slowly pulling the door shut. I hide in the back stall, standing on the toilet seat and crouching down. My heart pounds. I can't get enough air. *They can hear me gasping*, I think. I try to hold my breath. I pray. I'm amazed by what I just saw—Heitor pointing a gun at an unarmed man.

"No—" Juvelino cries again.

Gunshots. Too many to count. Both guns. Automatics. Then I hear the other guy—not-Heitor—laughing. "*Vamos,*" he says.

The door slams shut. The vehicle drives away.

I'm frozen there. I start to sob without making a sound. I know I have to get out, but I can't face the sight of what they did to Juvelino. I force myself. From the bathroom door, I see a smear of red down the chalky white wall behind the desk. I go for the front door. Juvelino is slumped over in a pool of blood. It looks purple on the shiny blue floor. His legs are folded under him sideways at a sharp angle—a pose that would hurt the living. His eyes are wide open.

I cough and my eyes water. I crash through the door. I run around the corner and up an alley. I hear a siren blocks away and approaching fast. I keep to the same side street I took to get there. I break the quiet, running and gasping all the way back to the apartment.

Motion lights go on again. A huge *fila*, a Brazilian mastiff, stirs. It jumps at the flimsy chain-link fence that stands between us. It's taller than me up on its hind legs like that, and it drools and barks and snarls in a gravelly double bass. I keep running.

I creep into the apartment, change out of the missionary outfit, and lie on my mattress. I can still hear Lilly's voice in my ear. I replay our conversation. I don't sleep. *No,* Juvelino cries. *Filho de puta,* the guy with Heitor says. Gunshots and laughter. Acrid gun smoke taste comes back to my mouth. I sob again silently. Nordgren doesn't stir.

Chapter Two

THE SMELL OF BLOOD gives Detective Costa heartburn. He keeps clearing his throat. Coughing. He leans against the wall and checks his watch. His eyes follow the small fan on the blood-stained desk as it oscillates. Countless black flies land on the corpse and hold there until the fan completes its cycle, blowing them airborne again.

Costa's hair is thinning on top. He is tall—maybe six three—and thick. He plays defense for a police-league *futebol* team with no regard for his body or anyone else's. He wears a small gold crucifix around his neck that was given to him for working on a special security detail to protect Pope John Paul II when he visited Brazil fifteen years back. Costa's eyes are brown and permanently tired.

A man in his late twenties pulls up in front of the Opa on a bike. He drops the bike and runs inside. His rumpled clothes, bed head, and droopy eyes say he just woke up. His T-shirt says

Mamonas Assassinas, which translates to either "Killer Boobs" or "Killer Big Boobs," depending on how picky one is about things like that. Mamonas Assassinas was a band that earned its cult following the old fashioned way—by dying in a tragic plane crash before its legions of fans realized that it sucked.

"Where the hell have you been?" Costa says.

"Out partying."

"Typical."

"Yeah," Assis says. "A night club called my bed. Small, but all kinds of atmosphere." He pulls an aluminum case out of his backpack. He carefully removes a camera and a lens from the case.

"That's not the only camera in Brazil," Costa says.

"I'm your only partner," Assis says. He attaches the lens, cleans it, and starts shooting. He gets a few wide shots, and then he zooms in. The face. The legs. The blood. The bullet shells littered across the shiny blue floor.

Costa watches impatiently. He crosses himself. Then he crosses the room in three broad steps. He stands over the corpse.

"Get this." Costa points at an intricate blood stain sprayed on the wall.

"Abstract expressionism," Assis says. "You have a good eye."

Costa ignores Assis. "And these." He points at deep bullet pocks in the plaster wall. "Why are you standing way over there? Can you get it from there?"

"Can you get any closer?" Assis says. "Maybe lie down next to him? I can't get both of your heads in the frame."

"Laugh it up," Costa says.

"Smile," Assis says, snapping a picture of Detective Costa glaring back at him. "Good. Now chin up. Suck in that gut."

"All right. All right." Costa steps back.

"Just a few more," Assis says. He moves closer. Costa watches as he zooms in tight on Juvelino's chest. Entry wounds. Tiny black holes. More blood. "That should do it. Unless you two want to get in a few more."

"I'm good," Costa says. "We're good. Both of us."

Assis pulls the lens off the camera. He packs both camera and lens in the aluminum case, which he returns to his backpack. Careful not to spoil any fingerprints, Costa fishes the pale bullet shells from the floor one by one with a pencil and deposits them into a plastic sack. There are twenty, maybe more. He closes the sack and balances it in his hand.

"Doesn't make any sense," he says. "At close range. In this little shop. Gun standing about here. Corpse behind the counter. Why shoot him like a zombie that wouldn't stop coming?"

"It's a shame," Assis says. "So many wasted bullets."

Costa tosses the bag of spent shells at Assis, who catches it awkwardly. Costa has to get blood on his shoes to get close enough to pat the corpse down. There is blood dripping from his fingertips by the time he pulls a wallet out of the dead man's back pocket. He raises an identity card to eye level, and blood runs down his sleeve.

"*Juvelino Neto Melo da Silva*. Actually sounds familiar, you know? But I can't place him." Costa puts the identity card back and tosses the wallet to Assis. Then he bends over and carefully wipes the blood from his hands onto Juvelino's pants.

"Add one more to the list," Assis says. "*Drogas*."

"It doesn't have to be drugs," Costa says. "Why drugs?"

"It's always drugs."

"Yeah."

"People are resigned to it. Except you, apparently."

"What about this guy's family—somebody won't be resigned to this."

"They know the score. Drugs and thugs, amigo. His family can only care as much as the *traficantes* let them."

"So Juvelino here is from the *favela*? And this is some traficante cracking down?"

"What else have you got?"

"Say somebody has a beef with the phone company."

"No," Assis says. "He was competition. He was dealing out of this place, and this just happens to be somebody else's territory. At a minimum he owed them money."

"Sure," Costa says.

"And he could have been a junkie. Just look at him."

"Maybe he was a cop."

"Now we all have second jobs?" Assis says.

"Said the part-time wedding photographer."

Costa and Assis sweep the place for evidence as they talk. They check every drawer. Every odd corner.

"More than anything else," Assis says, "this part of the job reminds me of what I really wanted to be."

"A full-time wedding photographer?"

"No."

"A traficante?"

"Getting colder."

"Help me out here."

"A civil engineer," Assis says. "I always notice what kind of a building somebody died in. You remember that guy last week? Outside the monastery?"

"No."

"And I have this recurring dream that I'm somewhere ancient. The Parthenon or something. And there are dead bodies all over the place. I just step over them. All I can see are columns and relief sculpture."

"My partner is one weird cop."

"And look at this place!" Assis says. "It's the opposite of architecture. Maybe thirty or forty years old. And how do they fix it up? Blue plastic! Olinda is full of these cheap cinderblock jobs."

"Why didn't this guy have the good sense to get shot in the Parthenon?"

"An earthquake would crumble this place to dust," Assis says.

"An earthquake?" Costa swallows the acid in the back of his throat. He coughs and laughs at the same time. "We don't even have earthquakes."

"It would," Assis says. "Guaranteed."

They find no drugs. Not much money either. There is some cash in Juvelino's wallet and a few bills in the little blue plastic desk, but only about twenty *reais* total. Nothing in the eyes of even the most hopeless traficante. Certainly nothing worth getting killed over.

"Look at this," Costa says. He pulls a yellow bed sheet and a pillow out from under the desk. "Can you imagine Juvelino here sacking out on the floor? Catching himself some shut-eye in the early morning hours?"

"He certainly wasn't sitting here all night with a gun on his knee under the table."

They go through papers from the desk. There is a call log. Somebody signed in at 11:00 p.m., and then the last name on the list signed in at 12:35 a.m. The clock on the wall says 1:53 a.m.

"Take that down," Costa says. "Zach Carson."

"Yes sir," Assis says.

"Sounds English, right?" Costa says. "*Americano*? You think Zach is male or female?"

"Sounds *macho* to me."

"Wait for them to come get the body," Costa says. "Then shut this place down. Nobody—especially phone company people—comes in here. Get a fingerprint guy over. Order up a list of calls made out of here in the last twenty-four hours. Incoming calls too, I suppose. Get me this Zach person's information. Have the *Polícia Federal* run the name."

"That all?" Assis says.

"That should keep you," Costa says. "I'll be in bright and early. Don't call me tonight. I mean it. If something comes up, you just sit on it until morning. If there's a real emergency, I want you to go ahead and call your mother."

Chapter Three

Elder nordgren's alarm goes off. I'm still wide awake. Still staring at the ceiling. I have been trying all night to think of Lilly, but it's no good. I try to picture her face again. I try to hear her laughing. To smell her perfume.

We hiked up Big Cottonwood Canyon to Lake Blanche on our first date. We talked for hours—she was funny—and she climbed the trail like a goat, except the word *goat* doesn't quite capture it. I often treasure the memories, a complete mental scrapbook, of the view of her hiking ahead of me on the trail. I try to picture the lines her legs made in those jeans and hiking boots. I give up. Even Lilly's legs can't chase the image of *Juvelino dead on the floor* out of my mind.

I stop fighting it; I try to think my way through what happened and how I ended up at the Opa last night in the first place. I start at my decision to call Lilly and work backward. The fact that I don't talk much about certain things carried me to the Opa.

For example, I haven't told Elder Nordgren—or anybody else in Brazil—that my parents' divorce just became final. My mom sent me a letter a few weeks after I got to Brazil announcing that my dad was now living in Las Vegas with his girlfriend.

This was not quite the surprise that she thought it was. It was a relief. I was tired of pretending that I didn't know.

The real surprise—that my parents had sold the house I grew up in—came in a letter from my mom about two weeks ago. The letter had a new return address, and it consisted of two full pages of gushing about the carpet, blinds, and countertops in her new condo. She promised to send pictures. Also, she informed me that it was a one-bedroom, and that I should plan on moving directly from the mission to a college dorm somewhere. She mentioned in passing that she had saved a few things from my old bedroom. These things were in a single box in a storage unit with everything else that didn't fit in the condo.

I wrote her back, but I was too angry to ask her exactly what she saved from a room full of books and music and trophies and pictures and nonmissionary clothes. I wrote my dad that week too, but I didn't bother asking about my stuff. I didn't have to. Saving my stuff would have required basic awareness that other people exist, a mental state that my dad almost never achieves. It was like a natural disaster had destroyed all evidence of my childhood. Except worse in my mind because you don't take an earthquake personally. An earthquake didn't give birth to me.

Losing all this—my childhood home, my stuff—made me homesick. That's where Lilly comes in. Don't get me wrong; I sincerely care for her. But she has become something more than a girlfriend. She is home. The only thing left waiting for me back in Utah that my parents didn't donate to the thrift store. The thought of Lilly has been my escape from all kinds of unpleasant things, and I have thought about her a lot since my mom's letter last week. So—last night—I decided to call her.

"You snooze, you lose," Nordgren says on his way to the shower.

"Live it up," I say. "Save some cold water for me."

"You sick, dude?"

"I'm all right."

"You're a different shade of pale this morning."

"Thank you."

Nordgren closes the bathroom door. I get up, throw on clothes, and grab my phone card. I don't go back to the Opa for obvious reasons. I go in the opposite direction to a pay phone. Some Brazilians about my age in board shorts and flip-flops pass in front of me. They walk casually toward the sound of the crashing waves, each with a wildly colored surfboard under his arm. I dial Presidente Ford's cell phone, a number missionaries call only in emergencies. I feel a hand on the back of my neck.

"What is it with you and phones, Elder Carson?"

"Heitor," I say. Before I baptized him, Nordgren and I spent hours teaching Heitor and his family. He'd said he was planning on serving a mission just like us, and he said it again last night at the little party—only hours before he gunned down Juvelino.

"So who are you calling?" he says.

"Nobody." I push his hand away from my neck and glare at

him over my shoulder. "Missionary stuff." He has the same scared look on his face he had last night. He is in the same clothes. *The gun*, I tell myself. *He still has a gun on him.*

"Hang up."

"Why?"

"You calling the cops?"

"No."

"Your presidente? Your people back in the States?"

"Come on, man."

"Hello," Presidente Ford says. "Hello?"

"This is Elder Carson," I say.

"Good morning, Elder. Is everything all right?"

I look at Heitor again. "Yes," I say.

"What is it, Elder?"

"I just wanted to tell you—about a family we are teaching."

"Yes?"

"We're very excited—they'll be baptized soon."

"Good!"

I hesitate.

"This number—I'm always happy to talk, Elder—but I need you to remember that this phone is for emergencies. Don't forget, there are 248 of you."

"I understand. I better go—in that case—good-bye, Presidente Ford."

Heitor grabs the receiver and slams it home. "We need to talk," he says, eyeing an old man across the street, who is opening up a *caldo de cana*—sugarcane juice—stand for the day.

"I don't think so," I say.

"We're going to talk. Not here. Let's take a walk back to your apartment."

"I'm not done using the telephone."

"That's what we need to talk about. You won't be making any calls for a while."

I turn around and look him in the eyes. "Are you threatening me, Heitor?"

"Do I need to threaten you?"

"We were friends. You made us believe you were going on a mission!"

"I'm sorry, Elder Carson."

"You're sorry?" I start walking. He follows me back home. I open the apartment door, and he pushes his way in. I don't resist him.

"Tell me about this family."

"What?"

"On the phone just now."

"They're great people. What do you want to know?"

"Of all the places you could have gone last night," Heitor says. "The Opa?"

"That guy," I say. "The one you left all over the floor—"

"Your mouth is going to get us both killed."

"Is that what you came here to tell me? It turns out that you're a murderer in your spare time, and I should be discreet about it?"

"What were you doing at the Opa last night, Elder? You guys never use the phone! And twice now in twenty-four hours?"

I shrug.

"That can't happen, Elder Carson. If you decide that you just have to talk to someone about last night, understand this: you will wind up dead. Maybe not just you. Elder Nordgren. Maybe other missionaries too. And me and my family. Do you have any doubts after last night?"

"It feels like you're threatening me again, Heitor."

"Does it?"

"We were tight, man. We were brothers."

He doesn't acknowledge that. His left hand falls on a copy of the *Liahona* on the kitchen table. He picks it up and casually turns the pages. "Where is Nordgren?" he says.

"He's taking a shower. Is that all right?"

"You told him, didn't you."

"Why would I, Heitor?"

"Does he know?"

"Of course he doesn't know."

"Let's keep it that way."

We glare at each other.

"His name was Juvelino," I say.

"You think I don't know his name? Why do you care? Trust me, he had it coming. Jesus himself couldn't help little old Juvelino."

"Heitor," I say. "I taught that guy."

"So you taught him. Big deal. That guy was a loser. Forget him."

"He had a heartbeat. And eyes. And parents. He was a child of God! Were you even in the church long enough to get that reference?"

"Preach, Americano."

"You're breaking my heart, buddy. This isn't you."

"I like you guys. You know that. I had fun doing the church thing with you. It did my folks good to see it. I don't have any regrets. My mom thinks I'm just like you now." He laughs. "She thinks I'm saving up for a mission!"

"Because that's what you told her! Why would you do that? If this is who you are, Heitor? Why pretend?"

"Do you think I like this?" He pulls out his gun. "That this is how I want to take care of my family? That I have some other choice? You guys came around, and, for a few days, I let myself think I could actually get away from it all. Start again. Have a new life." He puts the gun in my ribs. "To not have to carry this around. To forget that some *capanga* like me will eventually shoot me in the back—and that I'll deserve it."

"You have a choice."

"What do you know?" he says, returning the gun to the waistband of his shorts. "You're just some rich Americano passing through. My family needs the money. And even if they didn't, I know too much now. These people won't let me just walk away. They would kill me just for thinking about leaving them."

"You better go." I open the door. "This is a lot for me to take in. I always thought that—I thought I could see it in somebody's face if—"

"If they were damned?"

"If they were completely without the Spirit," I say.

"Whatever," he says.

"Yeah—well—I didn't see it in you. But I think I see it now."

Heitor puts a finger on my chest. "Remember, amigo," he

says. "You don't know anything. You never left your apartment last night. You have a little white book of rules, and you keep *all* of them."

"Good-bye, Heitor."

"Listen to me," he says. His voice cracks. I can see fear in his eyes. "These people will *kill* you. They'll probably make *me* kill you. I don't want to do that. Last night—if they knew—that's what I'm supposed to do to witnesses. Nothing stops these people. They have money and power you wouldn't believe."

"I won't say anything."

"Don't forget that I gave you another chance last night. You owe me. Do you understand?"

"Go," I say.

He goes.

I sit on my bed. I stare at my hands and think about what I should do next. My mind races aimlessly.

Nordgren comes out of the bathroom in a towel. "Who was at the door?"

"What?"

"You were talking to somebody."

"Magazines—" I act casual. "Just some kid selling magazines. Pushy little guy wouldn't take no for an answer."

"You've got to hate people going door to door like that."

"I know."

"Giving people their pitch. Shilling their books and magazines and such."

"What kind of people do that?"

"No offense, but you look terrible. You sure you feel all right?"

"Yes."

"I'm going to make some pancakes. What do you say? My mom sent me some maple extract—"

"All right."

I can see all three of Nordgren's tattoos. There is a stylized Polynesian sea turtle on his left arm. And a little black wave crashing on his right shoulder blade. And an orange sunburst on the side of his left leg just above the knee.

"Is that a yes on the pancakes?" Nordgren says.

"Yeah. Sounds good."

I hit the shower while Nordgren puts on the missionary outfit in the other room and makes breakfast. Even in the shower, I can smell the homemade syrup as he melts sugar in a pot and adds the maple extract. After that comes the smell of homemade pancakes burning in our only pan.

Nordgren and I get along even though we are exact opposites. He decided to hate me before we ever met—he actually told me that—but he couldn't sustain it. I'm a district leader, and apparently I have a reputation in the mission for insufferable qualities like intensity and obedience. Missionaries who know me would never believe that I went out last night alone. They especially wouldn't believe I went out to call Lilly. Once, I had a companion tell me that I reminded him of the missionary training center. He assured me that this observation was not a compliment. I'm not that bad, really. But I don't go out of my way trying to change people's minds about me. Why bother?

Nordgren has a reputation for things like his mastery of Brazilian slang and his exhaustive knowledge of the mission's hundreds of miles of white sand beaches. Don't get me wrong. He loves the people, and he loves to help them any way he can. He's a good missionary. But he never really planned on serving a mission in the first place, and he has an allergic reaction to all the picky little rules, the neckties, and the missionaries—like me—who take themselves too seriously.

Nordgren doesn't have a dramatic repentance story. By his account, he is an average surfer and an above-average guitarist. For about five years before his mission, he fronted the third-best surf-ska-reggae-punk band in San Diego. He doesn't have a single premission picture of himself without straw-colored curls halfway down his back. To hear him tell it, he got bored with that life. An endless party doesn't feel like a party after a while. It gets tedious.

He went to church one Sunday with his mom, just for variety. He went again. His third week back after years away, the bishop told him he had six months to decide whether or not he was going to serve a mission before he was over the age limit. A few weeks later, Nordgren broke up with his girlfriend, and he left his band. He didn't cut his hair until the night before he left for Provo. And he never bought a proper tie. I didn't even know they made clip-ons for grown men until I got assigned to work with Nordgren.

After two and a half months together, Nordgren and I have discovered a few things we have in common. We both like to throw ourselves into pick-up futebol games in the middle of the street. The kids use rocks or green coconuts to make goalposts. Sometimes they don't even have a real ball—just a roughly spherical mound of rags or tape. Also, we both hate the relentless pressure we get from mission leaders to produce big numbers. Nordgren just blows it off and tries to be like Jesus. For some reason, I grit my teeth and try to please the people up the chain of command. It usually works out, though; I think we balance each other.

I finish up, get dressed, and we eat the pancakes. I still can't get the smell of gun smoke and Juvelino's blood out of my mouth. I'm already tired of trying.

Chapter Four

Zone meeting starts two hours later. All the missionaries in Olinda meet at a church every Friday morning. We are a matching set: short hair, dark slacks, short-sleeved white dress shirts, conservative ties, and identical black rectangular nametags clipped onto our left breast pockets. Seven of us are from the States, and the other five are Brazilians. The Americanos are mostly from Utah. The Brazilians are *paulistas, cariocas,* and *gauchos*—city kids from São Paulo, Rio, and Porto Allegre. They consider northeastern Brazil almost as exotic as the Utah boys do.

We sit in a semicircle facing a green chalkboard. We report our results for the week by entering numbers into a big grid. We track things like the number of lessons taught and the number of people each companionship managed to bring to their ward's Sunday services. The most important number—the only one that really matters—is convert baptisms.

Two missionaries serve as zone leaders. They stand at the chalkboard and interpret the numbers. There is some praise for big numbers. Mostly they patronize and humiliate the missionaries who had a bad week.

Nordgren and I recently figured out that people from Olinda use the term *zone* to refer to the part of town where the police don't enforce laws against prostitution. For months, we had failed to understand the odd looks we got when we talked about going to zone meeting or why a woman on the bus—she overheard our conversation about a new zone leader—informed us that *she* was a zone leader too and that we were welcome to patronize her establishment anytime. She assured us that we would be very popular. She even promised to cut us a deal.

Right now, one of the zone leaders is speculating to the entire Olinda zone about whether the mediocre statistics Nordgren and I compiled last week are the product of insufficient faith, personal unworthiness, laziness, or maybe a combination of all three. I usually don't just sit there and take stuff like that, but today I'm finding it hard to care. Instead, I replay to myself everything that happened the day before. I wish I could go back to before *Juvelino dead on the floor*. Back to before *Heitor with a gun in his hand*. The day before is far away now, like cold cereal and the feeling of carpet under my bare feet—trivial comforts I didn't expect to miss so much when I left the MTC for Brazil.

I try to piece together the part before *Juvelino dead on the floor*. It was our only day off for the week. Nordgren and I spent the morning in the old part of Olinda touring ancient churches. Then it was basketball in Recife with Presidente Ford, groceries, and back to the apartment to do laundry and write some short letters home. P-day ends at 6:00 p.m. Then it's back to work.

Yesterday at about 6:15 p.m., Nordgren and I were back in the missionary outfit making our way to a little party. A family we baptized last month—Heitor's family—was getting together with a family we are planning to baptize this month.

A kid on the street came up to us. He looked us over.

"What's up?" I said.

"Are you airline pilots?" the kid asked.

"Why would pilots be walking down *this* street?" Nordgren said.

"Why wouldn't they?" the kid asked. "What's wrong with my street?"

"It's a very nice street," Nordgren said. "So yeah, this place is probably just crawling with airline pilots."

"We're not pilots," I said. "Sorry."

Nordgren and I turned up a narrow cobblestone road, this kid still following us. The beach, a grove of palm trees, and a busy highway were all behind us down the hill. We were on a twisting, narrow old lane, not far from the Opa I would visit later that night.

We had learned about the history of this hill on a previous day off. Indigenous people called the hill home before the Portuguese settled it almost five hundred years ago. First the Portuguese chopped down all the brazilwood in sight. Then they started up sugarcane plantations. Slaves were imported. Priests too: Jesuits, Franciscans, Benedictines, and Carmelites. We understood that Mormons—who didn't arrive in Brazil until the 1920s—are rank newcomers compared to the rest.

Descendants of planters and slaves still live here. Nordgren and I have met people who claim both. The priests' descendants are still here too. Their churches and monasteries occupy the top of the hill. There is a nice view from up there. Beyond the thick canopy of mango and guava and cashew and papaya and palm trees, you can see miles of white sand beach. And miles and miles of blue-green sea. Recife—sprawling and modern; the answer to Olinda all these centuries later—stretches across the entire southern horizon.

Nordgren and I passed ancient row houses on both sides as we climbed the hill. They were pink, blue, yellow, and white. They cast long shadows, and their broad shutters usually yawned open—no glass—to permit ventilation. Most of these openings have come to be secured by thick iron bars much newer than the houses.

The music changed from one house to the next. Music is always playing here. Radios everywhere endlessly pound out the beat of *carnaval*: *axé*, *choro*, samba, *frevo*, and *pagode*. Troupes of drummers play street corners for money. Neighbors jam together on porches. Choirs sing praises and monks chant off in the distance, safe under cloisters at the top of the hill. *Macumbeiros* feverishly drum and invoke *Iemanja* and a host of other West African deities. Flatbed trucks with huge speakers mounted on back blare slogans for deodorant and politicians.

Nordgren and I got to the party, and this kid was still with us. "Hey amigo, you coming in or what?" Nordgren said.

"Yeah!" he said. "Thanks!"

The kid sat quietly in a corner while Nordgren and I added

what we could to the noise. Nordgren played a traditional English tune on a guitar that the local bishop had brought. The entire group sang the cumbersome Portuguese translation of an already cumbersome nineteenth-century Mormon hymn.

Heitor was there. His full name is Heitor Milton de Oliveira. I know that because I filled out the record-of-ordinance form for his baptism. Heitor is eighteen, and he lives with his parents Alberto and Teresa, his grandma Lucia, and his two little sisters Aurelia and Renata. I baptized all six of them.

Starting into the second verse, I looked across the room at them. Heitor had his arm around Dona Lucia and little Renata. The two of them each had a hand under the dark green cover of a hymnbook. They seemed to bask in the attention he paid them. Heitor, oblivious to their adoration, sang with a booming voice, joyful and off-key. He always had a broad, confident smile.

People are drawn to Heitor. We first contacted his family working door to door on a Saturday afternoon. Even on that first day, Nordgren and I knew that he was the kind of guy we wanted on our team. We guessed that if he took an interest in the church, his entire family would follow. He did, and we were right.

We saw in Heitor the potential to realize a dream. Most missionaries are not remarkable. We muddle through; we serve as well as we can with the gifts—however meager—God gave us. But we hope that some lasting good may come from our efforts. That the things we do will ripple across space and time to bless many lives. Nordgren and I would do only so much in the time we had left. Heitor seemed to have a personality that would make him a better missionary than either of us would ever be. The ripples he would make, we hoped, would wash over generations.

The third time we visited his family, Heitor started asking us if he could serve a mission. From then on, we imagined him converting hundreds. And returning home with honor. And getting married and having children with broad, confident smiles and sending them out on missions to convert hundreds more.

After the hymn and opening prayer, we watched a church movie: *Juntos Para Sempre*. Dessert was mango juice and yellow cake full of chunks of caramelized pineapple. Our little guest from the street ate three pieces.

The party was all but over. It was time for me and Nordgren to start our walk back home. I was standing there by the door ready to go with my backpack on. Heitor came over to me. I shook his hand and told him that he would make a great missionary. I predicted that he would get sent to São Paulo. Santos maybe. Or Campinas. Both missions where friends of mine are serving.

"We'll see," Heitor said. "Maybe I'll get sent to Utah."

"You never know," I said. "Maybe you'll get sent to Tokyo."

"I know it won't be easy," he said.

"It's not for the faint of heart," I said. "But you're up to it."

"Leaving won't be easy," he said.

"Why is that?"

"I'll miss my family."

"Serving a mission is the best thing you could do for your family."

"I have a girlfriend."

"I do too," I said. I pulled my scriptures out of my backpack and showed him the picture of Lilly taped inside the front cover.

"She's cute," Heitor said.

"No," I said. "She's *hot*."

"Not bad for an Americana," Heitor conceded.

"Whatever," I laughed.

Heitor examined the picture. "You really think this sweet little tomato is going to wait around for *you*?"

"She'll wait," I said.

"What makes you so sure?"

"I write her letters," I said. "Every week. Dude—girls like letters. It's old-fashioned and romantic."

"If you say so," Heitor said.

"I do."

"You guys only get to call home on Christmas, right?"

"And Mother's Day. It's not as bad as it sounds, Heitor. Your girl will wait for you. And if she doesn't—well, a returned missionary is a hot commodity around these parts. Lots of young women in the church around here are looking for a good man."

"How would you know?"

"That's just what I hear."

"Relax," Heitor said. "I'm going. There are just a lot of things to take care of. I have a job—my family depends on me."

"You do?"

"Don't act so surprised," Heitor said.

"I'm not surprised that you take care of your family, Heitor. What do you do?"

He hesitated. At the time, I just assumed he was embarrassed by whatever form of unglamorous occupation he practiced. Then he said, "I work at a restaurant."

"Which one?" I said.

"Recife," he said. "South side. Outside your mission boundaries, I think."

"It doesn't matter. You can always get another job. You can get a better job. The world is full of restaurants."

"I'm going," Heitor said. And he reached out and ran his fingers over the white inset lettering of my name. "São Paulo is a long way away."

"It would be good for you," I said. "Travel a little. See the big city."

"Exactly," he said.

Two minutes later, I was talking to Heitor's dad.

"Do you have one of those little phone stores in Olinda somewhere?" I said. "Somewhere I can make a little call home? Don't rat me out here—I have a reputation to uphold among the faithful."

I fast-forward now—I'm still just ignoring zone meeting. I come to Juvelino. I see the vacant look in his eyes. The last thing before *Juvelino dead on the floor* was Lilly. The sound of her voice and a flood of unbearable sweetness. And a lot of memories I can't reach now. Things like holding her. Kissing her. Making plans for our future together. For the first time, I think about the possibility that I might never see Lilly again.

Chapter Five

Luz de Sá is doing shots of *Pitú*—sugarcane whiskey—and watching a telenovela. Luz is well into her forties. She has had her share of plastic surgery, but it has been a while since she could afford to freshen things up. Still, she has a perfect suntan, which is free if you can get yourself to the beach.

Her apartment is white and green. White walls. White floor. White faux-leather couches. Green curtains. Jaunty green blobs of modern art in white frames. And plants everywhere: palms too tall for the ceiling, huge fiddle-leaf figs, vines with garish, fragrant orange flowers.

She hears somebody pounding next door. She knows instantly that something is wrong. That is the Americanos' apartment. They visit everybody, but nobody ever visits them. Once Jehovah's Witnesses knocked on their door. It made her laugh for some reason—she expected fireworks of a religious fanatic nature—and she ran to her bedroom to get her camera. The JWs were leaving when she came back. The Americanos apparently invited them in, but the JWs refused. They gave the Mormons nothing but some *Watchtower*s and a view of their backs.

Luz opens her door and sticks her head out. She eyes a tall man, strong, balding. A good-looking side of beef, in her eyes. He ignores her. She notices two more things about him: his solemn, confident eyes and the cross around his neck. She guesses that he is probably too Catholic to be much fun, but she doesn't let that discourage her. Not yet anyway. Because people can change.

He tries the doorknob. He puts his shoulder hard into the door and tries the knob again. The door almost gives. The jamb makes a distinct cracking noise.

"Hey," Luz says. "What is this? You breaking in here?"

"This doesn't concern you," he says. "Disappear."

"There's nobody home there anyway. And nothing worth stealing. You're wasting your time, meu amigo."

"Who lives here?"

"Not you," Luz says.

"Thanks."

"I'm calling the police."

"Detective Costa," he says, going toward her. He gives her his card and an ironic smile. "Consider me called."

She examines the card.

"Looks fake," she says.

"Oh yeah?"

"Anybody could have cards made up. You probably hand these things out all over town. I bet they go over big with the ladies."

"I've got fake keys to a fake jail cell," he says. "You want me take you there right now in my fake police car?"

"Luz de Sá," she says. She tucks his card in her bra and offers him her hand. She imagines him kissing it like a prince in a movie. He only shakes it politely.

"Can we talk for a minute?" Costa says.

"Are the boys in trouble?"

"I don't know. Maybe. I have to check up on something. We're talking about the Americanos, right?"

Luz opens her door wide and gestures for Costa to come in. She leads him to a hard, white, low-slung rectangle of a couch. Costa looks around. "It's a jungle in here," he says. "And it smells like a drunk sleeping it off on the bus station floor," he adds under his breath. Luz just smiles and offers him a slug of Pitú.

He says no, but she pours him one anyway. He frowns. "I'm on duty," he says. He takes the glass and steadies it on his knee. She sits across from him. She studies the dark rings under his eyes. She doesn't notice at first that he is staring down the TV like it has insulted his mother.

"I hope you don't mind the background noise." Luz gestures at the TV, remote control in hand. "I'm really into this."

"No problem," he says. "Who else lives here?"

"I have a cat," she says. "Galileo."

"Great."

"I call him Leo for short," she says. "He thinks it makes him sound ferocious."

"Sounds like a really wonderful cat. No family? Other than the cat?"

"Divorced. My kids are grown."

"How long have you lived here?"

"Look, this is about the boys, right? Because I'm clean. Unless it has recently become illegal to poison my brain with telenovelas and Pitú."

"It's about the boys. How long have you lived here?"

"I was born here."

"You were born in this apartment?" he says.

"You're the detective," she says. "You tell me."

"I'm not here to fool around."

"That's too bad." Luz gives him her best reckless leer. "You sure about that?"

"How long?" Costa leaves her cold.

"Four years in March. But I'm a natural-born child of the beautiful and historic Olinda. I was born in the hospital. Are you *Olindense*, officer?"

"That's detective," he says. "Yeah, I'm from here."

"Then I'm proud to know you," she says.

"Fine. Tell me about the boys."

"They're Americanos."

"How long have they been around?"

"Longer than me and Galileo," she says. "Different guys, of course. Every few months, one leaves and another one comes to take his place. They always make the switch on a Wednesday. At least two of them have been here all along. There were three of them for a while last year, but it didn't last."

"Have you noticed anything unusual about them?"

"Yes."

"What?"

"Everything."

"Like what?"

"Have you ever been around them? At twenty, my son was good for nothing. He only ever exerted himself on top of a surfboard or a girl."

"They don't surf much?"

"It is God seven days a week with them."

"Did anything ever happen with these Americanos that made you worry about your safety?"

"No—they are very nice boys," she says. "Super nice. Weird nice."

"Do they have any enemies?"

"I don't know! The people from the other churches? The *crentes* or whatever? The Jehovah's Witnesses?"

"Other than that?"

"No."

"Anything else you want to tell me about them?"

"Of course, they're religious fanatics. But quiet too, you know? Gone all day, quiet at night. Ideal neighbors, I guess. But with a lot of religion mixed in. It's kind of hard to explain."

"Do you know one called Zach Carson?"

"I know Elder Carson," she says. "They're all *Elder* something."

"Apparently *Elder* isn't really his first name."

"That's what I'm telling you. It's like a title. Like *ancião*. Maybe you should write this stuff down."

"What do you know about him?"

"He's the taller one right now. Handsome. Not that it does me any good. He's a baby. He's not all grown up like you."

Costa gives her a tired glare.

"Elder Carson has short hair," she says. "Sandy brown. Blue eyes. Walks like a robot. Wears a tie and a dingy blue backpack everywhere he goes."

"Anything else?"

"That's about it. I mean, we've had our debates about the world. I try to be friendly up to a point. So every time a new Mormon comes to town, including Carson, he tries to convince me that I have a soul."

"Right. Other than that—"

Luz reaches up behind her and plucks a leaf from a vine climbing up her wall. The leaf is roughly the size and shape of a ping-pong paddle. Its flesh is dark green—almost black—and waxy. The broken end oozes white. She sniffs at it with pleasure. Then she holds the leaf out to Costa. "This is all I believe in," she says. "The physical world. Matter. Life. There is nothing else. Nothing."

"Good for you," he says. "Everybody believes in something."

"Or nothing."

"Nothing is something."

"Do you?"

"Do I what? Believe in something?"

"Do you?"

Costa lets it go. The last thing he wants to do is encourage her. He just looks at her blandly.

"I'll tell you another thing about those boys," Luz says. "Sometimes I think they are just like Coca-Cola and the CNN."

"I don't get it," Costa says.

"Just that this place has been colonized plenty. I don't go in for religion. But especially not Americano religion."

He slowly raises his glass of Pitú to her. Not a toast. More aggressive than that. "It doesn't take much *cana* to get you going, does it, Dona de Sá?"

"Good conversation is good conversation," she says. Her face flushes red. "You think I'm drunk? I try to help you, and you insult me?"

"Good conversation!" Costa laughs.

"This is nothing." Luz tries to get back her composure.

"Do you know a man named Juvelino Neto Melo da Silva?"

"More questions?"

"I appreciate that you are in the middle of a telenovela here."

He looks up at the TV. A man hidden behind a curtain watches a couple kiss passionately.

"*Nossa!*" Luz says. "These two have been fooling around for weeks now. Finally the old man gets wise."

"This is—" Costa says, "what do they call it on TV? *Official police business*. So if you don't mind."

The man behind the curtain pulls a long, narrow knife out of his sock. An arch, sinister look comes over his face. The music swells. The telenovela cuts to a commercial.

"What was it, again?" Luz says, her eyes still fixed on the screen. "Juvelino de what?"

"Juvelino Neto Melo da Silva."

"I've never heard of him. Who is he?"

"I don't want to take any more of your time. You've already been so helpful. What else can you tell me about Elder Carson?"

"Nothing."

"In that case—"

"So what did Carson do?"

Costa raises the Pitú to his nose. He sniffs. "You should have told me how much I was going to need this," he says. He gulps it down.

"It was implied," she says.

He hands the empty glass to Luz.

"Is this about the Elbow?" she says.

He gives her a *boa tarde*. "No," he says. "The man you call the Elbow is in prison." Costa lets himself out, brushing cat fur off his pants as he goes.

Chapter Six

WE GO BACK to our area after zone meeting. On the way, Nordgren and I stop at a bakery for some *pão doce* and *guarana*, rolls stuffed with passion-fruit jelly and sugary soda pop brewed from a little red berry that grows all over the rainforest. Twice a day—early in the morning and around four in the afternoon—the many corner bakeries around Olinda expel possibly the sweetest smell in the world: fresh-baked bread. For some reason, it reminds me of the smell of a certain detergent or fabric softener (or whatever) from home. That is the smell that comes to me when I think about home. Someday I'll probably think of my time in Brazil and the smell of fresh-baked bread will come back to me.

We eat. There is a futebol game on the TV high on the wall behind the counter. Flamengo and Gremio. The baker cheers loudly for Gremio because—he tells us—he hates Flamengo and especially its fans. Flamengo scores a goal. The baker curses. He turns off the TV in protest. He slams the remote control down on the counter. Two minutes later, he turns the game back on.

Nordgren and I watch a big guy in jeans and a T-shirt come in the front door. He is balding, and his eyes have black rings under them. He doesn't approach the counter. He pulls a chair up to our table and sits down.

"Elder Carson?" he says, looking both of us over.

"Yeah," I say. "What's up?" My heard pounds; I realize he may be a thug tied to Heitor. And that he might try to kill me.

"*Polícia Civil*," he says. "Detective Costa."

"Pleased to meet you." I hold out my hand.

Costa looks at my hand. He shakes it after an amused pause. "I have a few questions for you," he says.

"That's what I like to hear." Nordgren pulls out his daily planner. "Like big ones?"

"I hadn't thought of them in terms of size."

"The big ones are our specialty." Nordgren pats his backpack. "Like, who are we? Where did we come from?"

"No."

"No?" Nordgren says.

"My questions are not that big."

"That's all right. We would still love to sit down with your family sometime and share our message. Can we set up an appointment?"

Costa gives him a grim smile.

"What?" Nordgren says.

"Look, son, I need to talk to your friend. Just me and him. Do you mind?"

"We stay together," Nordgren says. Cops have approached us before; they just wanted to see our identity cards. He gets out his wallet and shows Costa his card. "Check our documents if you want. It's all good with our papers."

"This is not about documents."

"We stay *together*," Nordgren says. "If this is something serious, maybe we should call our mission presidente."

"It isn't serious," Costa says. "Not yet anyway. Not for you."

"We have rights," Nordgren says.

"Take it easy," Costa says.

"I want to call the U.S. consulate," Nordgren says.

"Why would you need to do that?" Costa says.

"You aren't *really* a cop, are you," Nordgren says.

"Come on," Costa says. He produces a card and hands it to Nordgren. "Of course I am. I just need five minutes with your friend here. Don't be a nuisance."

Nordgren stands up. Costa stands too. Nordgren takes a step into Costa's personal space. Nordgren hasn't hit anyone since before he became a missionary. But people threaten us, throw garbage at us, insult us in vile and personal ways—and I have seen Nordgren resist the urge to take a swing. I realize he might be on his way to losing control for the first time in Brazil.

"Prove it," Nordgren says. "Or get the hell out of here. This card is a fake."

"Really?" Costa laughs in Nordgren's face. "Maybe we should both get out of here. I'll give you one free shot before I break you."

I get up fast and put myself between them. I give the bakery a quick once over with my eyes. Everyone has stopped what they were doing; their eyes are fixed on us. "Give us a minute," I say to Nordgren. My heartbeat pounds in my ears.

"I'm not leaving you, man."

"We won't leave the bakery. Just let him talk to me. No big deal—"

"You sure?"

"Yeah."

"I don't have good feeling about this."

"Five minutes," I say. "It's all right."

Nordgren goes across the bakery. He watches anxiously from under an old black-and-white poster of Pelé mid–bicycle kick.

"Where were you last night?" Costa says.

I hesitate. I decide to lie, because I believed Heitor when he said that talking would get me and others killed. Also, I don't know if I can trust Costa. I don't know if he can protect me if I talk. I realize he might decide that I killed Juvelino just because I was there when it happened.

"Well?" he says.

"We work until nine thirty. Bedtime is ten thirty."

"What about last night?"

"That's every night," I say.

"It never changes?"

"Nope. The rules are strict."

"You sure?"

"Yeah," I say. "That it?"

"One more thing," he says. "Do you know a man by the name of Juvelino Neto Melo da Silva?"

I don't say anything.

"Well?" he says.

"I know a guy named Juvelino," I say. I look over at Nordgren. "I don't have a clue about 'Neto Melo' and all the rest of that."

"Oh yeah?" Costa says. "Tell me about your Juvelino."

"I met him the same way we meet most people around here. Elder Nordgren and I showed up at his house uninvited a few weeks back and offered to teach him a lesson about Jesus."

"What does he look like?"

I see Juvelino as he was last night—slumped over, blank eyes wide open in a pool of blood. "A little shorter than me," I say. "Skinny guy. Dark hair. Mustache, I think—very thin. Nothing unusual, really. Older. Sixty, maybe seventy. I don't know."

"Dark skin or light?"

"Not very dark," I say. "In the middle."

"What else can you give me on his appearance?"

"That's all I can remember."

"You said you went to his house, right? Where does he live?"

"It's not far," I say. "An old house on the hill. Halfway up."

"Yeah," he says. "So was Juvelino with you Mormons?"

"No," I say. "He wasn't interested. We did our best, but—"

"You visited him a lot?" he says.

"No. Probably only once. No, it was twice. We always leave a copy of the Book of Mormon with people. We go back at least once and see if they took any interest in it. He didn't. We let him keep the book anyway."

"What did Juvelino do for work?" Costa says.

"He—" I stop.

"Yes?"

"No idea."

"You were going to say something."

"I misunderstood at first. My Portuguese isn't great."

"I was going to compliment you," Costa says. "It's good enough. What were you going to say?"

"Nothing."

"You have anything else you want to tell me?"

"Nope."

"You were at home in bed last night after ten thirty, right? You were in bed all through the night?"

"That's right," I say.

"Where do you live?"

I give him the address. He leaves.

Nordgren returns to our table. He doesn't sit. He and I watch Costa through the window. He gets in his car, a shiny silver hatchback.

"Everything all right?" Nordgren says.

I look up into his sea-blue eyes. I try to make myself lie again. My throat tightens, and I feel sick deep in my stomach. "No," I choke out.

"What's going on?"

I look away out the window. Detective Costa sits there behind the wheel of his car. He looks right back at me. I feel a chill. *Trouble*, I tell myself.

"Elder Carson?"

"I need to tell you something," I say. I break away from Costa's gaze. I turn to face Nordgren again. "Do you remember teaching an old guy named Juvelino about a month ago?"

"No."

I sink a few inches into my chair. I look at my hands. "We taught him a first discussion. He lived on the old hill about halfway up. Skinny dude." I look up at Nordgren; he waits for me to finish. I look out the window again. Costa's hatchback pulls away. "He wasn't interested."

"Right, right."

"I saw something."

Nordgren sits down. His hands spread flat on the table. "I'm chained to you twenty-four-seven. How did you see something without me knowing about it?"

"Last night. I couldn't sleep. You were comatose. I went out."

"Out?"

"Yeah."

He leans in. "Where?"

"The Opa on the Rua do Sol."

Nordgren blinks two, maybe three times. "Why?"

"I called Lilly. I was just—it was stupid—I was missing her."

The baker cheers. Gremio has scored on a corner kick.

"I thought it would be good to hear her voice. I wouldn't have—you know—if I could go back. Obviously I didn't know—all this—"

"So the cop. You knew exactly why he wanted to talk to you."

"Yeah."

"And you played dumb. And *me*. When were you going to tell me about this?"

"I wanted to keep you out of it."

"Too late, bro!"

"I know. I thought not knowing anything would be safer for you."

"Safer?" He leans in even closer. "Safer? Are you trying to put me at ease when you say stuff like that?"

"No."

"So spit it out." Nordgren leans back in his chair. "What did you see?"

"I went to the Opa. I called Lilly. I was feeling great. I went to the bathroom before heading back. And I heard a car pull up outside. Some guys came in, and I could hear them saying something to the attendant. Juvelino—he was the attendant. I could tell something was wrong. Juvelino was like *No! Please!* So I opened the bathroom door to see what was wrong, which was crazy, right? Why would I do that? And there were two guys facing Juvelino; I was looking at their backs. They had guns on him. One of them—you're not going to believe this—one of them was Heitor."

Trouble and amazement flash across Nordgren's face. "*Our* Heitor?"

"Yeah."

"He looked right at me. At first I thought I was dead, but then I saw something in his eyes. He was scared. He gave me this look like *Get out of here!* I went back in the bathroom, and then there were gunshots. Then the door slammed and the car drove away. I ran for it. Juvelino was dead."

"You should have told me." Nordgren rubs his eyes. "I mean, you should have woken me up. Dude!"

"I thought I could keep you out of it. Nobody knows I was there but Heitor."

"We need to call the presidente. We need to get out of here."

"I tried calling him while you were in the shower. Heitor showed up at the pay phone. He must have been watching our place. He came up behind me before the call even went through."

"Dang!"

"I know."

"You couldn't have called her in the middle of the day sometime?"

"I know. You probably would have been cool with that."

"Yeah. I mean—*yeah!*" he says, clenching his fists.

"Only I wouldn't have been all right with that. I wouldn't have let myself. It was the kind of thing that only seems like a good idea late at night. And I couldn't sleep. I couldn't stop thinking about her."

"You couldn't have called her from some pay phone where there's no attendant to get murdered while you were there?"

"It's surprisingly easy to think of stuff like that after you accidentally witness an execution."

"Is that a joke?"

"I've been thinking of stuff like that all morning. Before I called her, I actually thought the store would be safer than standing out on the street at some pay phone in the middle of the night."

Nordgren expels a slow, even breath. His fists unclench and stay unclenched; he seems to regain control of himself. "I've been surfing out here, Elder Carson. *Surfing!* Not even on P-day or anything. I've gone with some members to two different nightclubs in Recife. It was hot chicks everywhere. Even I wouldn't just take off alone in the middle of the night."

There is a long pause.

"I'm sorry. Knowing what I know now—every part of what I did was stupid."

"Stupid is an understatement."

"What should we do?"

"What did you tell the cop?" Nordgren says.

"Cops around here scare me about as much as the criminals. Would you spill your guts to that guy? He's investigating a murder, and he probably thinks it would be a great career move to pin it on some Americano kid. I told him we had a quiet night at home."

"Is that all?"

"I told him that we know Juvelino."

"We need to call the presidente. We have to get out of here. We should get as far away as possible from Heitor and these cops."

"I'm sorry, Elder Nordgren."

"You don't have to say it again, dude. I know how you feel."

Chapter Seven

We have *feijão com arroz* for lunch with a family from the church every day of the week at noon. It is only eleven a.m. We go to our lunch appointment early. Sister Guimaraes, the Relief Society president, is not exactly happy to see us so early. She is busy cooking, cleaning, and soothing a teething toddler. We apologize and ask if we can use her phone.

"Something is wrong," she says. "Can I help?"

"We just need to call our presidente. In private, if that's all right."

"Sure. Absolutely." She gives us her phone and disappears back into the kitchen. Nordgren puts the phone on speaker and dials.

"This is Presidente Ford."

"Presidente, this is Elder Nordgren."

"Is Elder Carson with you?"

"Yes."

"I received a call this morning from Elder Carson. It was strange, to say the least. You two have been on my mind."

"Presidente"—Nordgren gives me a pained glance—"Elder Carson went out alone late last night."

"He did what?"

"Yeah. He called his girlfriend from a pay phone in a little shop. And he—well—he witnessed a murder while he was there. One of the men who committed the murder is a member of the church. A recent convert. He paid a visit—not the friendly kind—to our apartment this morning." I shake my head in disbelief; listening to Nordgren talk to the presidente makes everything seem somehow more real. "A police detective also found us in a bakery after zone meeting. He kind of interrogated Carson. I don't think we've seen the last of either one of them."

"Where are you now?"

"The Relief Society president's house. Our area."

"Get on a bus. Come straight to the mission office. Don't go back to your apartment. Forget about any appointments you may have. Do you understand?"

"Yes, Presidente."

"Do you have money for the bus?"

"Yes."

"I'll be here waiting for you. I'll call Salt Lake for instructions."

"Yes, Presidente."

"You boys are in danger. You know that."

"Yes."

"God be with you. Don't do anything stupid."

"Elder Carson already punched a lifetime's worth of stupid tickets," Nordgren says.

"That's right, son. Don't worry about that now. Just go. Go now."

We apologize again to Sister Guimaraes. We tell her she won't be seeing us for lunch. We run to the little Rio Doce bus station. It's about two kilometers away, down a series of narrow cobblestone lanes. We get to the station and check the schedule. The next bus that will get us anywhere close to the mission office doesn't leave for another twenty minutes.

"Restroom," Nordgren says after a few minutes of anxious pacing around the platform. I follow him. Coming out of the restroom a few minutes later, we see our bus. The electric sign above its matching broad, square windshields flashes BOA VISTA. We hurry to it. There is a short line; we are about three people from climbing aboard. A hand falls on my shoulder. I stop cold.

"Where are you going?" Heitor asks in a low voice.

"We have a meeting in Recife," Nordgren says.

"Not today," Heitor says. He gives the people behind us in the line a broad smile. "Go ahead," he tells them. "Please." Intent on paying their fare and claiming seats, people bypass me and Nordgren without interest.

"We can't miss this meeting," I say. "This is our bus."

"Apparently I didn't make myself clear," Heitor says. "You two don't go anywhere or do anything unless I say so."

"Just let us go," Nordgren says.

"Me going away is good for you," I say.

"I don't know," he says. "You had a lot to say to that cop."

"I didn't tell him anything."

"Maybe you didn't. I need some time to see what happens. I need some time to figure things out. That means you stay put. You just go on with normal missionary life. My friends and I will check on you."

Nordgren and I walk away from the bus station, Heitor walking maybe a hundred yards behind us. Eventually, not knowing what else to do, we act like missionaries. We work door to door looking for new people to teach, but we can't quite shake the uneasy feeling that Heitor is watching us.

Of course, we stick out everywhere we go. I'm almost as tall as Nordgren. Both of us are taller than the average Brazilian man by several inches. My hair is brown and his is blond, but we have the exact same haircut: number three with the electric clippers on the sides, number four on top. And we walk fast. We usually don't even realize we are doing it. I once turned around and saw a couple of kids imitating our gait and smothering laughter. They ran like we were going to hurt them or something. We just laughed and kept on walking, as stiff and determined as ever.

We make our way through a vast neighborhood of countless identical cinderblock houses. Some are well maintained with immaculate, lush yards. Some are neglected and filthy. Most are somewhere in between. All of them have tall cinderblock walls and steel gates that are conspicuously locked down. At each house, Nordgren and I stand outside the gate. One of us claps his hands three times. When I first came to Brazil, I felt strange standing in the middle of the road clapping my hands at peoples' houses. I got over it.

Occasionally someone opens their front door to greet us. More often, we hear a voice from somewhere inside scream, "Who is it?" At that moment—first contact—we don't do or say anything cute. We simply identify ourselves and offer to share a message about Jesus Christ. Most people reject us without the slightest hesitation. Some people curse at us. Once a guy chased me and Nordgren away from his house, swinging a tree branch at us. Apparently he kept it by his front door just in case we stopped by.

We finally get inside a house after an hour of exhausting humiliation. An hour made much worse by the fact that one of our recent converts is stalking us with a gun. We teach a young guy and his cousin who are tired from work. They are not interested.

"What should we do?" I say to Nordgren as we leave.

"Presidente Ford must be freaking out that we haven't showed up at the mission office yet."

"Will he send somebody to find us? Will he come?"

"It could be dangerous. We should have made that clear when we spoke."

"We need to think of something," I say. "Just act natural until we do."

It is more of the same after dinner. A lot of talk between houses about getting out of Olinda undetected. A lot of rejection on the street and in people's living rooms. A first discussion that goes nowhere. Then we get a young couple—Fernando and Marta—committed to be baptized. They are newlyweds.

Fernando is the assistant manager of a hotel in Recife. Marta is a college student. Fernando and Marta tell us that they had been looking for a church. Then we showed up in the street outside their small pink house. Nordgren clapped his hands, and Marta opened the door.

Nordgren and I walk back to our apartment for the night wearing twelve hours of sweat and dust. February is summer here, and it hasn't rained for days. The heat and humidity don't subside when the sun goes down. Especially on hot nights like this, quitting time is sweet. Our brisk pace usually slackens on the way home, and if we ever talk about something other than missionary work, this is the time.

We are quiet tonight. We come to an intersection. There are two old ladies in the middle of the road. One of them—she is taller with a hooked nose—has a chicken pinned by its wings. We stop and watch. The other lady—round, wearing a lacy shawl—moves in with a knife. She jabs it into the bird's gullet and then upward into the brain. The chicken doesn't fight. The women watch for a minute. Then the round one douses the bird with something. They step back. Then the tall one strikes a match and throws it at the chicken. The bird bursts into flames—it makes a column of fire maybe four feet tall. The women chant something in unison. I can't make it out.

"What the—?" Nordgren says.

They notice us. They glare. The round one spits a few sharp words in our general direction. A curse apparently, but I can't make heads or tails of anything she says. I don't think Nordgren can either. We continue on our way.

"That was messed up," Nordgren says.

"Yeah."

We are silent again. We cover the last mile home with haste. We climb the stairs to our apartment. We find Luz sitting on a white barstool outside our door. She is smoking a long brown cigarette, and she looks tired.

"*Boa noite*," she says.

We give her a couple of *boa noites* back. We stand there looking at her, waiting for her to move out of our way.

"Right—sorry." She moves.

I go to unlock the door.

"So what's new with you guys?" she says.

"Not much." I give her a tired smile. "Long day."

"Haven't seen you in a while," she says. She gives us a smile that I think is supposed to be warm and sincere.

"Our company is pretty easy to come by," Nordgren says.

"You can always stop by the church," I say. "We're there every Sunday."

Nordgren steps inside and flips on the light. He looks back at her. "We got the definite impression you weren't into—"

"The golden plates?" she says. "Moroni the angel?"

"Right."

"Yes, well, we are neighbors. And I thought I should tell you that some guy tried to get into your apartment today."

"Who?" I say.

"He said he was a cop. I stopped him. So you're welcome."

"Did he say what it was about?" I say.

"No."

"What did he look like?" Nordgren says.

"He was tall. Kind of sexy in an uptight way."

"What?" Nordgren says.

"Whatever," she says. "You guys were uptight sexy before it was cool."

"We're tired, Luz," Nordgren says, almost getting the door shut behind us. "Please spare us the comedy routine."

"Boa noite, Luz," I say.

"Are you boys in trouble?" Luz asks.

"We're fine," I say.

"You could be in more trouble than you think. Some cops around here can't be trusted. I don't want to make you boys worry, but—this cop, for example. He called himself Costa. You guys really don't know what he wants?"

"Maybe he was just hassling us because we're different," I say.

"You can't call everything that makes you uncomfortable persecution," she says. "He asked me all kinds of questions. He was after something."

"What?" Nordgren says.

"I don't know," she says. "But the last place on earth nice boys like you want to wind up is a Brazilian jail. They're human toilets. It could happen, though—if they think you did something serious."

"They would actually put us in jail?" Nordgren says. "But we didn't do anything! We're Americans! We have rights!"

"If I were you, amigo, I wouldn't go around saying things like that. Some people would lock you up and forget about you just to make a point about how special you are."

"Great," I say.

"Do you guys have somewhere you can go? Are there other Mormons you can go to? People who can help you out of a jam?"

"We have our mission office," Nordgren says. "Recife."

"I think you should go there."

"Good idea," I say.

"You should go *now*," she says. "The sooner the better. Buses still run for another hour or so. I'm even going to help pack your things."

"We already tried to get out," I say. "The bus thing isn't going to work."

"Why not?" Luz follows me and Nordgren into the apartment. We don't stop her, for some reason. It is a large studio. She sees dirty dishes and laundry everywhere. Beds unmade. There is an old table with chairs that don't match, and boxes of books by the door. And pictures of old white men in dark suits thumbtacked to the walls.

Luz points to a portrait of Jesus in a red robe on the wall. "Your Americano Jesus is very handsome," she says.

"Show some respect," I say.

"What happened when you tried to catch a bus?"

"You don't want to get caught up in this, Luz. Somebody stopped us."

"My friend has a car," Luz says. "I'll drive you to Recife. Vamos."

"Really?" Nordgren says.

"Thank you!" I say.

"Of course! You have suitcases?" She starts to empty out our closet. Suitcases. Shirts, ties, and pants.

"Leave our stuff," I say. "We should get going. On second thought, maybe Nordgren and I should wait here while you get the car. Is it close?"

"It's close."

Someone pounds on the door.

"Hide," I say to Luz.

"What?"

"We can't have a woman in our apartment."

She groans.

"Mission rules," I say. "This might be someone from the church."

She goes into the bathroom and shuts the door behind her.

I open the front door. It's Heitor. He pushes past us. He looks around suspiciously. "Boa noite," he finally says.

Silence.

"Heitor," Nordgren says. "What happened to you, buddy?"

"Don't do that," he says. "I'm not your buddy—"

"What do you want?" I say.

"I don't trust you."

"I don't know why not," I say.

"You didn't seem scared this morning when I left. I've been thinking about that all day long. And this is what I realized: I don't trust people who think they are righteous."

"I haven't said anything to anybody."

"I don't want to worry so much. What about tomorrow? What about the next day?" He lunges at me. Gives me a shove.

I'm not ready for it, and I tumble backward over my own suitcase.

Heitor kicks the suitcase. "What is this?" he says. "I thought we settled this."

I get up. I shove him back. He falls backward over the kitchen table. "You want to do this?" I say, stepping toward him. He climbs off the table and stands his ground. We are face to face now. Inches apart.

"Where are you going, Elder?" he says.

"What does it matter? I didn't see anything. I'm not talking to anybody. Can't you understand how this is good for you? This is perfect for you! You'll never see us again!"

"Tell me where you are going."

"I get it, Heitor. You came here to scare us again. For what, the third time today? Or did I lose track? Well, come on, tough guy!"

He takes a wild swing. His right fist finds my left cheekbone. A hard jab. But he is off balance—falling forward. I punch him in the nose. Blood pours down his face onto his white T-shirt. He tries to wipe it away, but there is too much.

"Where are you going?" he says.

"I don't know," I say. "Anywhere. Recife, for starters. Then maybe back home to Utah. That's a long way away, Heitor."

He takes another swing. Misses almost everything. I hit him in the gut. He doubles over and staggers back a few steps. Looks up at me. There are tears in his eyes.

"I'm sorry, Heitor. I love you, man. I didn't want to hurt you. You were going to be such a powerful missionary—"

"You don't get it," he says. "I wanted to serve a mission to get away from this life. If you hadn't seen me—"

"We just want to leave," I say. "We won't say anything, Heitor."

"I don't believe you," he says. "You will talk the second you get yourself a safe distance from here. And then I'm a dead man."

He pulls his gun from the waistband of his shorts and points it at my chest. "For the last time, Elder Carson, you are staying right here in Olinda until I say otherwise. You understand?"

"Whatever, man."

He lunges at me. Jabs his gun in my ribs. "I'm not joking! Don't think I won't kill you to save my own ass. Or Nordgren or anyone else. I'll pull the trigger without thinking twice. I saved your life last night in the Opa, and I saved it again this morning. Right now, man—you're still here—that means I just saved your life again."

"Not murdering people isn't the same as saving their lives," I say.

"It doesn't matter. I'm risking my neck every time I don't end you. And I expect some gratitude."

"Thank you," I say.

Heitor makes a sudden jerk like he is going to hit me with the gun. I flinch a little. He slaps me soft on the cheek with his other hand. "That's more like it," he says. "Fear looks good on you, Elder Carson."

He goes.

Luz comes out of the bathroom. "Who is he?" she says.

"Nobody," I say.

"I heard every word he just said," she says. "He's from your church, isn't he?"

"It depends what you mean," I say. "We recently baptized him a member of the church. We didn't really know him—obviously. This has nothing to do with the church."

"He's called Heitor de Oliveira," Nordgren says. He points at a list of recent converts on the kitchen table. We use it to track retention efforts.

"That's his address?" she says.

"Yeah," Nordgren says.

Luz goes for the door.

"Heitor," Nordgren says. "He could be out there. Watching."

She stops.

"The fire escape," Nordgren says. He and I help Luz climb over the grate that separates our fire escape from hers. Exhausted, Nordgren and I leave our suitcases gaping wide open on the orange-tile floor. We don't even talk. Nordgren, trying to read his scriptures, eventually dozes off. I get up and turn off the lights. I look out our window into the night. I imagine Heitor watching our apartment, seeing it go dark and wondering what it means. "Good night, Heitor," I say. I sleep too, but only after what feels like hours just staring at the ceiling and thinking about our next move.

Chapter Eight

THE NEXT MORNING, Nordgren and I get up at six thirty. We shower, dress, and eat breakfast by seven thirty. From seven thirty to eight thirty, we study the scriptures. From eight thirty to nine thirty, we study a chapter from *Preach My Gospel*, the church's instruction manual for missionaries. The same old routine. But both of us wear last night's sleeplessness on our faces. Both of us are preoccupied. There is no small talk. I'm thinking through what we decided to do today. So is Nordgren.

We leave our apartment at nine thirty. We walk fast. We don't stop until we are standing on the street outside Heitor's house twenty minutes later. It is small and neat. Cinder block painted off-white with deep-blue trim. A flowering vine with fragrant yellow blossoms climbs on the cinder-block wall encircling the entire lot. There is a banana tree in the corner heavy with fruit— tiny, dark-green stubs above; yellow crescent-tubes with black tips hanging below. The gate is closed and padlocked. Nordgren claps his hands. Heitor's dad, Alberto, appears at the front door in a clean blue jumpsuit, his name on a patch on the left breast pocket. He doesn't have his work boots on yet. Just heavy flip-flops that Brazilians call Hawaiians.

"Elders!" he says.

"Alberto!" we say. "Good morning!"

"Come in, amigos." He removes the padlock. "What a pleasant surprise!"

"Is it?" I say.

"Sure."

"We were worried it was much too early," I say.

"Of course not."

"Can we pay you a quick visit?" Nordgren says. "Looks like you're off to work."

"Sure. Sure. I always have time for you guys."

He seats us on the couch. "I'll get Teresa."

"Heitor here?" I say.

"He's working."

"Fair enough."

"I'll get the rest."

"Thanks!"

"You guys hungry?"

"Not at all. Just had breakfast."

We make small talk with Alberto and Teresa, Grandma Lucia, and Heitor's little sisters. Lucia is getting over a bout of pneumonia. Aurelia and Renata are playing on the same little-league futebol team.

Out of habit, we give them a spiritual thought. Elder

Nordgren reads them Malachi 4:6—"And he shall turn the heart of the fathers to the children, and the heart of the children to their fathers, lest I come and smite the earth with a curse." Nordgren briefly expounds on that—temples and how families can be sealed together for eternity across generations. We ask them if there is anything we can do for them. They insist that they are just fine.

"How is Heitor?" I fill in the first empty space in the conversation.

"Fine," Alberto says. "Busy."

"Sounds like this job keeps him hopping," Nordgren says.

"Yes," Alberto says.

"Where does Heitor work again?" Nordgren says.

"Some restaurant," Alberto says.

"It's not just work," Teresa says. "The poor kid is always studying! He takes the *Vestibular* in a few weeks. Do you understand what the Vestibular is?"

"Yes," I say.

"No," Nordgren says.

"It's like the SAT," I say to Nordgren. "A college admissions test, right?"

"Exactly," says Teresa.

"Heitor is going to college?" Nordgren says.

"Only if he aces the test," Alberto says. "That's how you get into the state schools, which are free."

"He is smart. He studies hard," Teresa says. "I can't imagine any other outcome."

"We've been worried about him," Nordgren says.

"Why?" Alberto says.

"Call it a prompting," I say.

"That's why we wanted to visit," Nordgren says. "You're sure everything is all right with Heitor?"

"What is it?" Grandma Lucia says. She slowly rubs her hands together. "There's something you're not telling us. This prompting—was it very specific?"

"No," I say. "We're just thinking about him."

"Does Heitor have friends—I mean, other than us? People he hangs out with?" Nordgren says.

"I don't know," Alberto says. "He doesn't have much time for hanging out between work, school, and the Vestibular. And now church on Sundays. Young Men on Tuesdays. Service projects. Scouts. The list goes on and on!"

We hear a motorcycle outside. Heitor. We hear the back door open and close.

"Hello?" Heitor says from the kitchen.

"In here," Teresa says.

"What's up?" Heitor says.

"Company," Alberto says. "Join us."

He comes around the corner. He stops cold on sight.

"Heitor!" Nordgren says cheerily.

"What are you doing here?" he says.

"Good to see you too," I say.

"Don't be rude, son," Teresa says. "We were just talking about you."

"I didn't expect company. And you guys—what a surprise!" He stares me down.

"Long time no see," I say.

"What were you talking about?" he says.

"Lots of things," Teresa says.

"We understand you've been studying," Nordgren says. "Big test coming up."

"Right," he says.

"What kind of stuff do you study?" Nordgren asks.

Heitor pauses. He gives me and Nordgren a menacing look. "The test covers many subjects," he says.

"Name one," Nordgren says.

"Don't be shy," Teresa says. "Our Heitor is going to be a doctor! After his mission, of course. It's a long way off—"

"Mom," Heitor says, acting embarrassed. "I really have to get back to work. Elders—we should talk more about this later."

"Sure," I say.

"I deposited my paycheck." Heitor turns to Alberto. "Tips have been good. It's a little more than usual. I didn't want you to worry."

"Very good," Alberto says.

"I have to go," Heitor says.

"See you tonight, son," Alberto says.

"Great to see you guys." Heitor turns so his family can't see him glower in our general direction.

"Sometimes we forget what a great guy you are," I say. "You will make a great missionary someday."

"Whatever." Heitor's fake modesty has an edge his family can't seem to hear.

"Whatever?" Alberto says, slapping Heitor across the back. "Elder Carson knows exactly what he's talking about!"

"Of course," Teresa says. "We were just reading a scripture. What was it? The Spirit of Elijah? You're going to help seal families together forever, just like the elders have done with us!"

...

After Heitor's house, we walk across our area to a favela called Ilha do Bicho, which translates to either "Bug Island" or "Devil Island," depending on who you ask. We expect to see Heitor around every corner. He can't be happy about our showing up at his house like that. We assume the people all around us are Heitor's friends. We eye every new face for some kind of recognition. We try to act natural.

Typical favelas are crowded, poor, dirty, and dangerous. They are discrete political units governed by traficantes. Gang violence and stray bullets can be daily problems in favelas. But other crime, which is bad for the drug trade, is rare. Drug-lord law enforcement is brutal and effective. Missionaries usually avoid favelas as a safety precaution, even though the traficantes rarely hassle us. Missionaries don't work door to door in favelas, but we sometimes teach referrals there. And we frequently go to the favela to visit other Mormons.

Despite their dark side, favelas have a certain dignity too. Ordinary working-class people, not gangsters or addicts, make up a majority of the people there. And many favela people are squatters. Their haphazard shanties—sometimes built one on top of the other six or seven stories high—display amazing ingenuity. Unfortunately, entire favelas have been known to slide down hillsides during particularly wet rainstorms, and favela fires are notoriously catastrophic.

Favelas also teem with music, color, and life. A majority of the musicians and dancers that make carnaval happen have their homes in favelas. Music is always playing there. Young girls are always dancing. Barefooted boys are always playing futebol. Like everywhere else in Brazil, lunch in the favela is feijão com arroz. Only, favela beans are stewed with more unusual cuts of pork: snouts, ears, hooves, and tails.

Some favelas are famous, like Rocinha in Rio and Heliópolis in São Paulo. People actually offer guided tours of those, guaranteed safe by the local drug cartel. By comparison, Ilha do Bicho is exceptionally squalid. No walking tours are offered.

Many of the dwellings in Ilha do Bicho are pieced together—right angles optional—with scraps of wood, sheet metal, and cardboard. Ilha do Bicho has roads, after a fashion. However, they are not paved, they are not straight, they are obstructed here and there by huge craters or unexcavated boulders, and the house numbers follow no logical progression. Sewage runs in open ditches adjacent to most roads in Ilha do Bicho. The odor is overpowering, and outsiders learn fast to be vigilant about where they step.

Nordgren and I go up to a shack painted powder blue, the late Dona Luiza's house. Elder Nordgren claps his hands.

"Who is it?" says a low voice from inside.

"It's us," I say. "The elders."

"What do you want?"

"Five minutes," I say. "Nothing religious. Guaranteed."

Mateus is not Mormon, but his brother, Marcos, is serving a

mission in São Paulo. We wait for Mateus to unlock the gate. We go in. The shack is tiny but orderly. Clean. There is a kitchen and two closet-size rooms. In the alley out back, the bathroom is a bucket in a plywood box that resembles a cheap coffin standing up on end. Pictures of the Virgin Mary hang on nearly every wall. Those are left over from Dona Luiza. She passed away a few months ago. I'm pleased that Mateus has not taken the pictures down.

"*Bom dia*," we say.

"You've got four minutes left," he says, eyeing us coldly. "What's up?"

"How is Marcos?"

"He's like you guys now, right?"

"More or less," Nordgren says. "Is that a bad thing?"

Mateus shrugs. He clenches and unclenches his forearms, and his snake-scale tattoos—dark green and blue—expand and contract.

I have been here in Olinda for five months, and I paid regular visits to Dona Luiza for the first three. She always insisted on feeding us. *An empty sack can't stand up!* she liked to say. Then we said, *You really don't have to feed us*. And we meant it.

Dona Luiza knew how to bake a cake, but accepting a slice felt like taking food out of her mouth. Yet we were unwilling to offend her by refusing her generosity. Then she said, *Try to stop me. Marcos is so far away. And do people in São Paulo feed him enough? You will eat for Marcos.* The juice was usually mango, passion fruit, guava, or *acerola*. Sometimes cashew, which is extremely sweet and sticks in your throat like glue. We ate. We thanked her profusely.

And when she turned her back, we hid small piles of bright green *real* notes under our plates. She would not accept it in any other way. Eventually, she sat down at the table and gave us a sad, beatific look. She was a perfect match—although much older—with the Mary behind her on the wall.

We rarely saw Mateus in those days. We got the impression that he worked a lot. If he happened to be around when we came to visit, Dona Luiza did everything she could to clear him out of the house, short of chasing him with a broom. We understood one thing about Mateus: he was a tough, tough guy. For some reason, Dona Luiza was always asking us to pray for him.

"Do you write him?" Nordgren says.

"Who?"

"Your brother. What do you mean, who?"

"I don't write him."

"You should," Nordgren says.

"Is that all?" Mateus says, getting up.

"We need your help," I say.

"What kind of help?"

"I saw something I wasn't supposed to," I say. "A murder, actually. And this guy—this guy has been following us around and threatening us. And a cop has been hassling us too. And these people—all of them—are watching us."

He is silent. He looks at the small expanse of tabletop between his hands.

"We need to get to Recife," Nordgren says. "We need to get to our mission office. And we can't just go catch a bus. This guy—"

"That's it? You want to go to Recife?"

"Safely. Without all these people knowing about it."

"How much?"

"What?"

"Fifty reais. That's how much it will cost you."

"Fifty?" Nordgren says.

"Take it or leave it."

"Fine," I say.

"Tonight. Meet here. Bring cash. Can you boys count to fifty?"

Chapter Nine

Luz can't sleep. She gets up and pours herself a drink. She thinks about Elder Carson mixing it up with Heitor. And she thinks about Detective Costa.

"Should I tell him?" she asks Galileo.

The cat is silent. Sound asleep. She strokes his fur all the same. She feels his slender rib cage slowly rise and fall under the weight of her hand.

"Will it help? Because I have to tell you, my love, I don't know what to do. Maybe he's dirty. I don't know." She yawns. She gulps down two more inches of Pitú and fumbles her way back to bed.

Still restless hours later, Luz gets up early. She has the headache and sour stomach she purchased the night before one shot of Pitú at a time. She walks to her friend's house and borrows his car. She drives to Heitor's address. It is a small house. Tidy. The blue paint on the door and shutters is fresh. She doesn't have a plan. She just sits across the street and waits.

She watches Elder Carson and Elder Nordgren leave. They stride quickly away down the street. A few minutes later, a man in a dark-blue jumpsuit comes out carrying an old-fashioned steel lunch box. He walks down the street and around a corner. A while later, a woman comes out in flip-flops and a tattered gold bathrobe. She sweeps the front porch, yawn-stretches, and goes back inside. A young man finally appears. Luz decides he must be Heitor. He is oblivious, with large headphones on his head. He gets on a motorcycle, kick-starts it, and speeds away. Luz follows him.

Heitor goes north to Jardim Atlantico, a nice neighborhood near Olinda. He pulls up to a graceful pink mansion on the beach. The top floor has three big windows facing the ocean. The windows on the bottom floor are smaller and protected by black wrought-iron bars. The driveway is lined with six tall royal palms. The mansion and the surrounding grounds are enclosed behind a tall wrought-iron fence.

Heitor punches in a code. He bobs his head, apparently to the music in his headphones. The driveway gate slowly opens. He goes in, kills the motorcycle, parks it, and lets himself in the front door. Luz parks across the street. Beachgoers have parked cars here and there up and down the entire street. The beach is mostly quiet. Weekday regulars—the elderly, the unemployed, and the odd teenager ditching school—sunbathe and search for empty bottles and cans and bob on surfboards waiting for waves.

After a while, a van pulls up and goes in. A tall blond man gets out. His face is sunburned bright red. He unloads three children from the van. Three little boys. They move slowly. All three of them in a row, heads downcast. The man has a pronounced limp. It makes Luz cringe just to watch him walk. They go into the pink mansion. Luz doubts that the children live there; their clothes are ragged.

Somebody pounds on the passenger window. Luz is startled. Then annoyed. A guy in a straw hat puts his face against the window. His big bloodshot eyes scan the car. He gives her a broad smile. He is tall and black and skinny. He has a big pink scar under his left eye in the shape of a teardrop.

"Coconut water right here," he says. "I've got *greeeeeeen* coconuts." He has a deep, booming, jolly voice.

"No thanks," Luz says. She winces and rubs her forehead. She digs in her purse and tries to collect herself.

"Nice and chilled." He gives her a big smile. "Coconuts right here!"

"Move on."

"Looks hot in that car, miss."

"No," she says. "Just no."

"Fit to soothe away that headache," he says, voice trailing off.

"Go away."

He pushes his cart up the street.

Luz sits there for hours. She tries to watch the house, but nothing happens. She gets bored and watches the beach. She falls asleep. She wakes up bathed in sweat and completely disoriented. She yawns and stretches and rubs her face. It all comes back to her. "What am I doing here?" she asks herself. "This is all wrong." She pulls a steel flask out of her purse, carefully unscrews the lid, and throws back a mouthful of Pitú. "Thank you, doctor," she says, wiping her mouth on the back of her hand.

The red-faced guy from the van finally limps his way out of the pink mansion, hefting a large white cooler. It looks heavy. He grunts and curses as he loads it into the back of the van. He leaves in a hurry.

The van comes back about an hour later. This time the guy has a girl, maybe fifteen years old, wearing black from head to toe. She looks a little too hard for her age. Luz doesn't like seeing her alone with him. *Where is your mother, little girl?* Luz asks herself.

The guy pulls her out of the van and shoves her toward the house. She trips and falls. He stands above her. He says something Luz can't make out. He makes like he is going to kick her. She stumbles to her feet and runs inside.

Luz writes down the address and the van's license plate number. She drives back to her apartment and gets her camera. She goes back, parks in the same general area, and waits.

The coconut guy comes back. As before, he puts his face in the window and peers in at Luz. He even smashes his broad nose against the glass.

"*Green* coconuts," he says. "How about it, lady?"

"Still no. Thank you."

"What gives, anyway?"

"You are a pest, aren't you?"

"Nobody comes to the beach to sit in their car. That's just a fact."

"Leave me alone? Please?"

"And you—you spent all morning here. You finally go. And now you're back! I don't get it!"

"If I buy a coconut, will you go away?"

"Sure."

"How much?"

"One real."

She rolls down her window and gives him a real. He stuffs it in his pocket. He digs a coconut out of his cart. He lops the top off with one blow of a very sharp machete.

"Keep it," she says.

"But miss," he says. He inserts a long, bright-pink straw into the coconut.

"I don't want it. I never wanted it. I just want you to go away and not come back."

"Now I feel bad," he says. "Here I am trying to make an honest living. I've got some mighty good coconuts here. Fresh, ripe, sweet, and cold." He sings the last part.

"Here's another real," she says.

"I couldn't take that."

"Please take it and promise me you won't come back. Just stick to the other side of the street, understand?"

He takes it. "There's nobody over there," he says.

"Leave me alone. Why is that so hard?"

"Are you all right?" he says.

"Are you an idiot?"

"Sure," he says. "Fine. Are you a cop or something?"

"Do I look like a cop? How many old ladies like me—yes, I'm a cop. You are under arrest for being a jackass."

"Sorry."

He goes down the street. He doesn't bother her again.

Eventually the guy from the van comes out. Heitor and a third guy—dressed in an expensive suit—are with him. They load the girl, one of the three boys, and some small pieces of luggage into the van. Luz gets pictures of all of them.

They leave. Luz waits for another hour. Nothing else happens. People are leaving the beach for the day. The sun is setting. Her borrowed car is one of the last ones parked on the street anywhere near the pink mansion. She goes home.

Chapter Ten

Before we go to meet Mateus, Nordgren and I keep an appointment to teach a young couple, Luiz and Dalia, who we met on the bus about a week ago. Walking to their apartment, we can't stop checking behind us. We look up and down every street and alley we cross. We keep expecting to see Heitor. We don't, and somehow that is worse. It makes us suspect every kid on the street. We want to see all of them as God's own children. And gods in embryo. Now all we see are potential gangsters sent by Heitor—probably with Glocks stuffed into the waistbands of their shorts and dirty switchblades in their tube socks.

The couple is all excited about joining the church. They are beautiful people, young and poor and obviously in love. Nordgren and I give them an hour-long discussion on the law of chastity. Nordgren awkwardly rattles off a list of prohibited carnal sins. Judging by their reaction, the phrase "sexual relations" as translated from the English is throwing them off.

"Do you understand what we're getting at?" I say.

"I think so," Luiz says. "I mean—" He makes an obscene gesture with his hands to indicate his comprehension.

"Yeah," I say. "Very good."

The guy chuckles. The girl glares at him until he stops.

"You're serious?" Luiz says. His eyebrows climb a full inch up his forehead. Further conversation brings out two important facts: Luiz and Dalia are not married, and they are no strangers to "sexual relations."

"We have good news for you two lovebirds!" Nordgren says. "You can still get baptized, but you have to get married first."

"I really want to do this," Dalia says. She gazes at Luiz with cow eyes. He tries to contain his hesitation.

"Just so you know," I say. "We have helped other couples get married before. You just go register at the clerk's office, pay the fee, and then show up for the ceremony. They marry off, like, twenty or thirty couples all at once. It's quick. Painless."

"Don't get *too* romantic on us here," Nordgren says. "Elder Carson is like a poet or something, isn't he? Going on like that about young love and such."

"That's just civil," Dalia says. "Can we do something in the church too?"

"Yes," I say. "The bishop does weddings. We could probably get people from the church to do decorations and cake and everything."

"Eventually you two can get married in the temple," Nordgren says. "Check this out." He produces a picture of the Recife temple from his backpack.

"That's three weddings!" Luiz says. "Or did I lose count?"

We explain about the temple. We finish up the discussion. We schedule another appointment despite our plan to disappear later that day. Luiz is visibly uncomfortable. His eyes are glazed over, and he is sunk back into the couch. Dalia is giddy and oblivious to him. She is off somewhere in her head working on her dress, cake, and flowers.

Nordgren and I leave. We walk toward the favela.

"This sucks," Nordgren says. "I can't believe we're going to miss that."

"Yeah," I say. "I'm really going to miss those people. People like them."

"We need to make sure somebody takes care of them," Nordgren says. "Remind me when we get to the mission office."

"I will," I say. I decide not to dampen Nordgren's spirits by asking him if he had paid any attention to the boyfriend's body language, facial contortions, and other expressions of general terror.

We would not usually set foot on Devil Island—Ilha do Bicho—at night. We get a lot of looks from people as we pass by. And people say things. *Check out moneybags and his brother. Hey, how many wrong turns does it take two white boys to get to Ilha do Bicho? Say something in English, you sexy loaves of bread!*

A kid maybe fifteen years old comes up to us. He lifts up his T-shirt a few inches and shows us the handgun tucked into his shorts.

"Mormons, right?" he says.

"Yeah," I say.

"Message from Heitor," he says.

"Who's Heitor?" Nordgren says.

"Cute," he says. "I'll tell him you said that."

"We're listening," I say.

"Luiz and Dalia," he says.

"That it?" I say.

"Heitor knows where you went today. He knows the name of every person you talked to. Including Luiz and Dalia. That's all."

"Tell Heitor that we love him," Nordgren says.

"You tell him," he says. "You'll see him again soon."

He walks away.

"Change of plans?" Nordgren says.

"No," I say. "Unless you have a better idea."

"No," Nordgren says.

We keep walking. We finally get to the blue shack where Mateus lives. It is dark—the door and shutters are closed. Nordgren claps. We wait. It is unusually quiet. Minutes pass. Mateus finally appears in the doorway. He looks both directions. Nothing. He lets us in. He has his hair pulled back in a greasy ponytail. His black tank top reveals more of his tattoos than we usually see.

"Opa," Mateus says.

Out of habit, Nordgren and I hold out our hands. Just like we are standing on his doorstep and he just invited us in to talk religion.

Mateus laughs, slow and deep. "You guys are too much," he says. "Such good manners!" He shakes our hands. "You two stiffs somehow managed to get the attention of the cops and traficantes?"

"Something like that," I say.

"You saw something, right?" Mateus laughs. "A little murder?"

We are silent. Mateus's sense of humor is wasted on us.

"You have the money?"

"Yeah," I say, digging in my backpack. "Here." I unfold a stack of green bills and flop them on the kitchen table. The rest of both Nordgren's and my allowances for the month got us to twenty-eight reias. The cash I'd set aside to buy souvenirs at the end of my mission—I had my heart set on a nice *berimbau*—covered the rest.

He gathers up the bills. Counts them slowly.

"It's all there," I say.

"Go get changed," Mateus says. "Marcos's things are in the back bedroom."

Nordgren and I go to the tiny bedroom to change. There is a small opening—a window without glass—behind crude wood shutters. There are some old shorts, T-shirts, and flip-flops in a pile on the bed. We start pulling off the missionary outfit.

"That guy gives me the creeps," Nordgren says.

"I know," I say.

"There are bad dudes. And then there is that guy."

"His own mother was nervous around him. You remember that?"

"Yeah."

"What are the odds Mateus earns an honest living?"

"I'm used to giving everybody the benefit of the doubt. But after the last few days—there's no way. None."

"Right."

"Listen," Nordgren says.

"What?"

"Somebody is out there with Mateus."

"You sure?"

"Back there," Mateus says.

There is another voice. I can't make out what it is saying.

"I know," Mateus laughs. "I told them to change."

The other voice again. I still can't make out words. It is low, sharp.

"Relax," Mateus says. "They aren't going anywhere."

"That doesn't sound good to me," I say.

"No," Nordgren says.

"Come on," I say, putting my white shirt back on. "Change of plans." I stuff my tie in my pocket. Nordgren does the same.

There is a knock at the door. We go silent. "Hello?" Mateus says. "You guys almost ready? Vamos, Mormons."

Nordgren is halfway out the window, his legs hanging there. Kicking wildly, he catches himself on the ground outside with his hands.

The knock becomes pounding.

"Just a minute," I say. "Hey, thanks again for offering to help us, Mateus. It means a lot." I go head first out the window behind Nordgren. "I just hope somebody will look out for your brother like this if he ever gets in a jam."

"Shut up," Mateus bellows. "Vamos! *Agora!*"

We hear Mateus crash through the flimsy door behind us. Nordgren and I run down the alley behind the house. It is a patchwork of colors and smells. There is garbage everywhere.

Most of the dwellings don't have indoor toilets, only numerous variations on the back-alley outhouse theme.

"You're dead, Mormons," Mateus calls after us.

We turn a corner. Nordgren crashes into a rusty old stove. He knocks it down and tumbles over it. Hundreds of cockroaches and three flabby rats scatter. I'm running directly behind Nordgren; I trip over a rat and hit the dirt. It shrieks and sinks its teeth into my shoulder. I reach around and pull it off—it's greasy and feverish-hot in my hand. I fling it away from me against a shack, pull myself up, and run after Nordgren.

We turn another corner. Nothing but the rough back walls of countless adjoining shacks. We can't see a way out.

"Give it up, guys," a voice somewhere behind us says. "This is our home. There's nowhere we won't find you."

We run until we reach a dead end. We can hear traffic on the street on the other side. We pound on the back doors of several shacks. Nothing. We try the doors, but they are all locked. I try to climb out of the alley. Nordgren gives me a boost. I get halfway up the side of a shack, and the thin sheet metal starts to buckle under my weight. I slide off carefully and tumble to the ground.

Nordgren finds a loose sheet of plywood and starts pulling on it. I grab on and pull with him. Nails pop loose and the plywood groans. We open up a hole in the back of a hovel. We squeeze in and pull the wall back into place behind us.

We pause. We can hear a TV in the next room. The music of carnaval. No matter how wretched, every home in the favela has a TV. Some have satellite dishes and hundreds of channels.

"Nothing sneaky now," I say. "Just haul ass out to the street.

Run to the first bus stop we see. Get on the first bus that comes. Ready? One, two, three—"

We go. We get a glimpse of middle-aged people copulating on the couch. They are big and sweaty and oblivious—they don't notice the Americanos running wildly through their living room.

Nordgren and I burst through their front door. The gate is locked, so we hop the fence. People in the street eye us suspiciously, but we can't afford to slow down.

"You all right?" I say.

"Yeah," Nordgren says. "You?"

"Fine—almost there."

"My eyes!" Nordgren says.

"That was extremely unpleasant."

"Understatement of the century."

"I don't think they even knew we were there."

"They didn't."

"The no-girls rule doesn't seem so bad sometimes."

"That's why we've got to get out of this, bro," Nordgren says. "The no-girls rule is one of the things I'm absolutely determined to outlive."

We gasp and laugh. We keep running for a while. We overtake a wiry old man in a straw hat pushing an old steel wheelbarrow heavy with *macaxeira*, brown tubers twice the size of potatoes. His load wobbles and almost spills as we pass him by.

"You see that bus stop?" Nordgren points. "Under the tree?"

"Yeah."

"Stop or keep running?"

"This is good."

The other people at the bus stop watch us. A short old lady holding a bag of green bananas. A couple of men with five-o'clock shadows in matching fluorescent green and pink samba-queen outfits—spandex, sequins, feathers. A few too many peekaboo panels expose tufts of short black hair for my taste. There is also a group of teenage girls all slutted up for carnaval.

"Go right to the back of the bus," Nordgren says. "Focus, dude. Almost there. And keep your head down. No big deal, right?"

"Just taking a bus into the city," I say. "It's P-day, and we're going to the mall. It'll all be over soon."

We hear a loud crack. Like a gunshot. The girls scream, and the old lady spills her bananas everywhere. We look around. Mateus and some other equally wholesome-looking guy are coming at us. Mateus has a gun in his hand.

We see some cops across the street. They are taking cover behind a car and drawing their guns.

"Over there," I say. Nordgren and I run across the street. Mateus sees the cops and does not fire. He tucks his gun back in his pants. He and his friend stand their ground and watch us intently.

"Detective Costa," I say to the cops. "Can you call him?"

"Who are you?" one of them says.

"Mormons." I point. "Those guys. We don't want to die."

"Is that right?" the cop says.

Two minutes later, Costa and his partner pull up in the silver hatchback. Mateus and his friend seem to recognize Costa. They seem to instantly lose interest in us. They turn and make for Ilha do Bicho. Costa's partner gets out of the car and shoves us into the backseat. We drive away.

Chapter Eleven

Traffic is heavy on the main highway. Costa goes fast anyway. He weaves in and out without any regard for other cars, street signs, or the lines painted on the highway.

"Will you take us to Recife?" Nordgren says. "To our mission office?"

"I'm Detective Assis. You know Detective Costa. We are Polícia Civil. We are going to the station."

"At least take us to the American consulate," Nordgren says.

Costa and Assis just look at each other. There is a long silence.

"New car?" I finally say.

"Yeah," Costa says. He acts like he isn't extremely pleased with it.

"I noticed it the other day," I say.

"It's his baby," Assis says.

"Why are people—bad people—chasing you through the

favela?" Costa says, glaring at us in the rearview mirror. "Because you guys didn't see anything, right? You didn't do anything wrong. You keep a strict schedule. Your keep all the rules."

We don't say anything. Traffic slows down to a crawl as we approach the old part of Olinda. Throngs from all over are coming to celebrate carnaval. They wear shorts and T-shirts or just shorts or just bikinis or just the bottom halves of bikinis. Some wear elaborate masks or tall white powdered wigs and pastel-colored colonial costumes. There are many women and drag queens in brilliant feathers of every color. There are a lot of clowns and a few grim reapers too.

"Where's the chicken?" Nordgren says.

"That's in Recife," Assis says. "The Midnight Rooster. You guys don't know the first thing about carnaval, do you?"

"We don't party much," I say.

"The Midnight Rooster is the mascot of the largest block in Recife."

"What's a block?"

"Blocks are clubs that party together," Assis says. "The Rooster has at least a million members. Maybe two million in a good year. Rio is all glitz and glamour. Recife has some of that too. Here in Olinda—we have the people's carnaval."

"What is it about Brazilians and chickens?" Nordgren says. "Remember those old ladies torching that chicken out in the street?"

"That was yesterday," I say.

"That was days ago," Nordgren says.

"I don't think so."

"*Macumba*," Costa says. "That's a standard hex. To curse somebody, burn a black hen in an intersection by the light of the moon. Sacrifice a white chicken at sunrise to reverse the hex. You can also bless a person's fingernail clippings to reverse a hex."

"That's crazy," Nordgren says.

"Maybe." Costa grins. "I pray to the Virgin Mother. Other people have their golden books."

"Is macumba real?" Nordgren says.

"I like my chicken fried with macaxeira," Assis says. "Feijão com arroz on the side. And plenty of beer. You won't see me out wasting a perfectly good *frango* like that."

We finally get past the traffic. We pull behind an ancient-looking yellow building with white doors and shutters. It is dwarfed by vast mango trees on both sides. The cops lead us through the back door and into a small room. There are a table and chairs, but no two-way mirror. Just a door and four blank walls. Assis offers us water.

"I don't want water," Nordgren says. "I want to go to Recife!"

"Does this guy ever get on your nerves?" Costa looks at me.

"I usually get on *his* nerves," I say.

"Are we under arrest or not?" Nordgren says.

"It doesn't matter what you call it, son." Costa says. "Your friend and I need to talk. This time we're going to really talk."

"Come on," Assis says to Nordgren. "This way, pretty boy." He leads Nordgren out of the room.

"This is your last chance," Costa says. "The night before last? Around midnight? Where were you?"

"I told you," I say.

"I don't think you did," Costa says.

"I don't have anything else to say to you."

"Are you scared?" he asks. "Stupid? What is it?"

I keep my mouth shut.

"The man's name was Juvelino Neto Melo da Silva."

"Right."

"You knew him. You had been to his house."

"I know."

"Did you exchange dollars for reais with Juvelino?"

"No."

"Did you ever place a bet with Juvelino?"

"No."

"Did you buy drugs from Juvelino?"

"I don't even drink coffee!"

"Some crackheads don't drink coffee."

"Do you really think I'm a crackhead?"

"Did you ever have a date with one of Juvelino's girls?"

"Of course not."

"Are you telling me you're not into girls or something?"

"Not hookers," I say.

"You knew Juvelino was a pimp?"

"You just told me he was, didn't you?"

"I just can't figure out how you Mormons made friends with this guy."

"I told you," I say. "We showed up at his house. He invited us in. We talk to just about anybody who will listen."

"That's another thing. The cops who called you in. They told us that one of the thugs chasing you through Ilha do Bicho was a guy called Mateus."

"Yeah," I say.

"How does he play in all this?"

"We knew his mom. A little old lady who passed away. Her other son is a missionary like us, but in São Paulo. Mateus is his brother."

Costa gives me a disgusted look. "Stay away from him. He's a psychopath. He hurts people."

"I believe you."

"Did Juvelino ever ask you to make a delivery for him?"

"No," I say. "Never." Then I laugh.

"What?" Costa says.

"Are you telling me that Juvelino did all that stuff? Hookers and gambling and—and deliveries?"

"I'm just asking," Costa says.

"Because if he was so busy—"

"What?"

"Why would he be working graveyard shifts at the Opa?"

"You tell me," Costa says.

"No idea."

Costa gets up and goes for the door. "I never told you that Juvelino worked graveyards at the Opa," he says. "I never said anything to you about the Opa at all."

I shut up again.

"Remember getting fingerprinted at customs? You left prints all over the Opa. The counter. The second phone from the back. The bathroom door. The bathroom."

I just listen. I don't have anything to say to that.

"I don't think you killed anybody," Costa says. "I think you're a liar. A bad one. As in not very skilled. I don't think you have murder in you. No offense, amigo."

Costa goes out. He comes back with some papers. He puts them on the table in front of me. The first is the Opa sign-in sheet. He points at my name, print and autograph.

"Zach Carson," he says. "12:35 a.m."

"Yeah," I say.

"The last name on the list," Costa says. "That's about the same time people called in the gunshots."

I look at the other paper. A printout with small type. I can't make any sense of it.

"Call records," Costa says. "You called a cell phone in Salt Lake City. Talked for ten minutes. Family?"

"Girlfriend," I say.

"Congratulations," Costa says.

"Thank you."

"This is what I keep telling myself," Costa says. "This kid saw something. Why else would he lie?"

"I didn't want to get in trouble," I say.

"Then talk," Costa says.

"No. I mean, that's why I lied. It was against mission rules to be out that late. It was against the rules to be alone. It was even against the rules to be calling my girlfriend."

"What happens if you break mission rules?"

"We have these big meetings," I say. "The guy in charge calls people out in front of everybody for breaking the rules."

"You are the target of a murder investigation—and you're going to lie to save face in front of the other Mormons?"

"What do you want me to say?"

"Tell me who killed Juvelino."

"I didn't even know he was dead until you told me."

"You saw nothing?"

"Nothing."

Costa just looks at me.

"I made my call. I left. Then you show up at the bakery the next day."

"That's it?"

"That's it," I say. "Will you let us go? Please?"

Costa grunts.

"I was in a hurry to get back. It was late. I was breaking the rules."

Costa is silent. He stands up and walks out. I just sit there. I'm shaking and exhausted. I sit there so long I fall asleep. I wake up hunched over on the table and drooling. My neck hurts. Costa is standing above me.

"Good morning," Costa says.

"It's morning?"

"I just mean welcome back. You didn't sleep *that* long."

"Can I go? Where's Elder Nordgren?"

"Here's the deal, kid. I can't let you go. I think you saw plenty. I think you know who killed poor old Juvelino."

"No," I say. "That's not—"

"Hear me out," he says. "I don't blame you at all for playing dumb. Between you and me, you are doing the smart thing.

People who volunteer themselves as witnesses around here don't exactly have long life expectancies."

"So let us go."

"I can't do that," Costa says. "Assis and I have talked it over. You are staying put. I want to take you guys straight to the airport and put you on a plane. That is, assuming your people can make arrangements. Maybe tonight. Maybe first thing in the morning. Just as soon as we can."

"Thank you."

"In the meantime," Costa says, "nobody—not even most of the people around this station—knows what's going on. If anybody asks, you two are suspected for the murder of Juvelino. Until we put you on a plane, this is a marathon interrogation."

Chapter Twelve

Assis returns to the interrogation room with Nordgren. "Hungry?" Assis says. He has a square white box and four brown bottles. It is a big pizza and very Brazilian. In addition to the usual toppings, there are sweet peas, sweet corn, and slices of hard-boiled egg. The bottles are off-brand guarana. Nordgren and I are beyond ravenous.

"I assume Detective Costa explained that you're safe here until we can get you out for good?"

"Yeah," I say.

"One more thing," Costa says, pointing his slice at me. "I talked with your presidente. I think he understands the situation. He is very concerned, and I don't think he was inclined to trust me. That is probably smart. I suspect he's on the phone with the American embassy right now. He'll do what he can to get you out of here despite us, but he also agreed to make arrangements.

Said he would get you two on the next flight available. He said he'll be in touch." Costa steps out.

"You guys all right?" Assis says.

"Thanks for the food," I say.

"I love this stuff," Nordgren says. "This thing is like the love child of an actual pizza and a freaking salad bar!"

"Thank you," Assis says. "Assuming that was a compliment."

"Of course it was," Nordgren says.

"I've seen guys like you around my neighborhood," Assis says. "The ties and all that. You're like priests, right?"

"Missionaries."

"You are celibate?"

"Pretty much," I say. "We don't call it that."

"So you go to clubs?"

"Not while we are missionaries," Nordgren says. "We're not supposed to, anyway."

"So you haven't been with any Brazilian girls?"

"Not the way you mean," Nordgren says.

"But you would like to if you could?"

"I would date a Brazilian," Nordgren says. "After the mission. Why not?"

"Exactly. Brazilians are the hottest women in the world. Am I right?" Assis punches me in the arm.

"I have a girlfriend," I say.

"Brazilians are hotter than Americanos," Assis plows on. "You can't deny that."

"That's probably true," Nordgren says. "I mean—no offense

to Carson's lady. There are some pretty girls back home. But we have seen some seriously hot Brazilians."

"What about you?" I say. "You have a girl or something?"

"Of course he doesn't," Nordgren says. "He only promotes Brazilian girls to young foreigners trying to walk the straight and narrow."

"Do you really have to ask?" Assis leers.

"Well, good for you," I say.

"I have a fiancée," Assis admits. "My player days are over. She wants a big wedding. I'm saving up, and it's going to be a while."

"Congratulations," I say, sincere this time.

"So you two will be priests forever?" Assis says. "This is your life? Your career?"

"No," Nordgren says. "This is only for two years."

"I'm going to college after this," I say.

"Big college man," Assis says.

"I'm going to be a dentist," I say. "Biology and then dental school."

"You want to pull teeth!" Assis says.

"Elder Carson dares to dream that dream," Nordgren says.

"I'm going to marry my girlfriend, Lilly," I say. "I'm going to build her a house. Red brick. Some kind of grand entryway with a staircase. Three-car garage. Lots of bedrooms fully stocked with children. And we'll never sell that place no matter what. It will always be there for them."

"How many kids?" Nordgren says.

"Five to seven," I say.

"*Caramba*," Assis says. "Seven kids?"

"What are you going to name them?" Nordgren says.

"I have some names I like—"

"This fantasy is very specific, isn't it," Nordgren says.

"What about you?" Assis says to Nordgren.

"I don't know," Nordgren says. "I play guitar. I might try to make a life of it. Maybe I'll go to college. Or start some kind of business. A restaurant or something. Music store. I don't know. I have another nine months of mission to work all that out."

"I don't get it," Assis says. "You guys have it pretty good."

"What don't you get?" I say.

"Why would you come here in the first place?"

"We came to Brazil because we wanted to," Nordgren says. "The church didn't force us. We believe in what we do." Nordgren gives me an unmistakable look. The look that means *Let's teach this guy a first discussion*. We do. It is a good one except for the fact that we don't have a copy of the Book of Mormon on us. We quote some passages from memory, and we promise to get him one later so he can check it out.

We finish, and Assis has to meet his fiancée for dinner. Alone now, Nordgren and I slouch in chairs on opposite sides of the table at the center of the interrogation room.

"I'm pooped," I yawn.

"Me too," Nordgren says. He stares at the floor. "I assume they have a toilet somewhere in this place, but I haven't seen it."

"Let me know if you do."

"Check."

"What time do you think it is?" I say.

"I think my watch is back on the bed at Mateus's filthy little shack."

"That was a nice watch."

"It was a gift from my ex-girlfriend. She wasn't too happy when my life took a sharp turn to the religious."

I go to the door and try it. No luck.

"I wish I was home right now. I mean *home* home," Nordgren says.

"I've had the exact same thought every day of my mission."

We laugh.

"But yeah, the last couple of days," I say. "I've been thinking about home. And wishing." I sit up straight in my chair. I rub my eyes. I look Nordgren directly in the eyes. "I feel like I should apologize again. I am sorry, Elder Nordgren. This mess is on my head. I've been thinking about your family. If something happens, I want them to know it was my fault."

"Drop it," Nordgren says. "Nothing is going to happen. Thinking like that doesn't help anybody."

"You are a freaking saint."

"Come on."

"You are, man."

"If it makes you feel better, I'm still pissed off at you. If we both survive this, I'm probably going to kill you."

"That's fair."

"So either way, it might all be over soon for you."

"That's the spirit."

There is a long silence. Nordgren and I don't even look at each other. We don't move at all.

"Do you want to say a prayer?" I finally break the silence.

"Yeah. We should. I mean, we just had companionship inventory, right? Are you calling on me?"

"Is that all right?" I say. "Either way—"

"I'll say it."

We bow our heads.

Nordgren prays. He thanks God for our health, our safety, and for the wealth and opportunities that we have enjoyed throughout our lives. He thanks God for the chance we've had to serve missions. He prays that God will watch over us and protect us, and that we'll return home in safety. He prays for our families at home, and for the other missionaries in the mission and all the people we are teaching. He prays for Heitor and his family. That Heitor's heart will somehow be softened, and that his family will be protected from all these gangsters and their guns. He prays that Heitor can somehow escape the life he has chosen. Finally, he prays that the trouble we are in won't harm the work. He closes the prayer. We both say amen.

I give Nordgren a nod that means thank you.

"We're going to make it out of this," Nordgren says.

"I appreciate you saying so, even if we don't," I say.

"We are protected. Trust me."

A guard opens the door. He looks like he weighs maybe three hundred pounds. He wears a gentle smile. He drops some blankets and pillows inside the door. "It might not seem comfortable," he says, "but this room beats our holding cells. Detective Costa asked me to look in on you."

"Thank you," Nordgren says.

"You need anything?"

"Bathroom," we say in unison.

A few hours later, the same guard opens the door. Nordgren sleeps peacefully. I'm wide awake. The guard gathers up the empty pizza box, empty brown bottles, and as many oil-soaked napkins as he can. He doesn't notice the small black object under a left-behind napkin: Assis's cell phone.

"You guys all right?" he says.

"Sure," I say, standing up. I lean on the table, my hand covering the phone.

"Is there anything I can do for you?" the guard says.

"We're good."

"Get some rest," he says.

I wait five minutes. Then I dial Lilly's number. It rings and rings and goes to voicemail. I hang up and dial her number again.

"Hello?"

"Lilly?"

"Who is this?"

"It's Zach. I told you I was going to call again. I kept my promise."

"Zach Carson?"

"Lilly?"

"This is Georgia. Lilly left her phone in my purse."

Georgia is Lilly's mom. She only tolerated me before the mission. I got the impression that she was extremely pleased to see me go. Particularly the part that involved my getting on a plane and flying thousands of miles away from her daughter.

"Oh." I hesitate. "Hi, Georgia. Can I speak with Lilly, please?"

"You are breaking the mission rules," she says.

I couldn't argue with that.

"And it sounds like this isn't the first time. Am I right?"

"Is she there?" I say. "It's important."

"The truth is—Lilly is grounded from her cell phone."

"Lilly's in college. She's grounded?"

"We pay for it. That is all the leverage we have left. I won't embarrass Lilly any more by going on about that."

"Please," I say. My voice is soft.

"Zach," she says. "I will tell her you called. Do you want to leave a message with me?"

"No."

"She's not here anyway, Zach. Should I have her call you? Is this your number?"

"No. This is a friend's phone. I don't even have a number here. I'll try again another time."

"Good-bye, Zach."

"Tell Lilly I love her."

She sighs. She is not pleased.

"Will you tell her that?"

"Good-bye, Zach."

"Bye."

The phone goes silent. I call my mom's cell phone. No answer. I don't leave a message. I try my dad's cell. Nothing. No surprise there—my dad never answers his phone and never calls anyone back. At least not his kids. He hasn't even written a letter in months. His voicemail is full anyway.

I call the home phone—the number I memorized as a child

just in case I got lost. My mom taught me how to tie my shoes around the same time. After several rings, I get the disconnected number message: *We're sorry. You have reached a number that has been disconnected or is no longer in service. If you feel you have reached this recording in error, please check the number and try your call again.*

I can't think of any other numbers to call. I can't come up with even an area code for any of my siblings. I call my mom's cell phone again. I want to leave a message, but I don't know what to say. The phone beeps. I hesitate, leaving nothing but the sound of me breathing and thinking. Finally I say, "I love you, Mom. This is Zach. I just wanted you to know." I hang up. I curse.

Chapter Thirteen

It is a bright morning. Luz de Sá is asleep on her couch. A dead bottle of Pitú lies peacefully by her side. The TV is droning softly. She rubs her forehead absently, groans, and rolls over on her back.

Galileo the cat is hungry. It jumps on the couch, climbs from Luz's feet to her chest, and turns. It slowly passes its long black tail across her face. Luz gets up, sending both the cat and the empty bottle tumbling to the floor. Only the cat lands standing up. Luz lunges at the bottle. Then she realizes it is empty. She stands up and stretches. She yawns, rubs her eyes, and gives the bottle a lazy kick.

"Bad cat," she says. "Bad, bad cat." There are two small green bowls on the kitchen floor. Luz fills one with water. The other she fills with cat food, which looks like breakfast cereal but smells like half-digested liver.

She has some coffee punched up with a slug from a fresh

bottle of Pitú. She showers and dresses herself in a bright yellow sundress. She pulls a big blue grocery sack out of the pantry, folds it twice, and tucks it under her arm. It matches her flip-flops perfectly. She goes, leaving the TV on behind her closed door, which she locks.

She rides the bus to the police station. The bus is crowded, but Luz manages to snag an open seat on the aisle. A few stops later, a woman of maybe sixty-five gets on the bus. Out of respect, Luz offers the woman her seat.

"Thank you," the woman says.

Luz stands. The woman hesitates. Others eye the seat with interest.

"Do you want it or not?" Luz says.

"I'm waiting for it to cool down." The woman shrugs.

Luz sits again. "I'll let you know if it does."

At the station, Luz demands to see Detective Costa. He makes her wait for a good half-hour before appearing in the small waiting room.

"*Senhora* de Sá," he says.

"Call me Luz."

"How's the cat?"

"Galileo is just fine. Thank you for asking."

"What can I do for you?"

"What did you do with the Americanos?"

"What did *I* do with them?" He gives her an incredulous grin.

"They didn't come home last night. If you don't know where they are, you better start looking for their bodies."

"I can't comment on an ongoing investigation, but I assure you that your Americano friends are safe."

"What investigation?" she says.

"The old man gunned down at the Opa the other night."

"What do those boys have to do with that?"

"Apparently those boys are your cat now?" Costa grins. "And you think they're stuck up in a tree?"

"So they are here? Have you been rough with them?"

"No more than usual," Costa says.

"Great," she says.

"I live to beat on kids. Can you blame me?"

"Did Elder Nordgren tell you that you have to treat him special because he's an Americano?" Luz says.

Costa laughs.

"*O, meu filho*. I told him not to be an ass."

"No," Costa says. "He didn't say that."

"Thank goodness. Can I see them?"

"No."

"Why not?"

"Because we don't have visiting hours for murder suspects under interrogation."

"Murder?" Luz says. "My boys?"

"We have evidence that Elder Carson was present at the time and place of the murder," Costa says. "We understand these guys never leave each other's side, so it follows that if one of them was involved, then both of them were. We have decided it is prudent to detain both of them."

"You obviously have things under control," Luz says. "Congratulations on locking up a couple of harmless puppies."

"Is that it, lady?"

"No," she says. "I have to tell you something about this investigation."

"This is a police matter, Senhora de Sá," Costa says. "You understand that these people are dangerous?"

"Some tough guy called Heitor came to their place the night before last."

"Go on."

"I was there," she says.

"Where?"

"I was in their apartment."

"What for?"

"I was hiding in their bathroom," she says.

"Of course you were."

"It's a long story. Look—I was there, and I heard everything. And this guy was threatening Elder Carson. And he was telling him to keep quiet. Said something about something Carson saw."

"So?"

"So why do you think people like that are coming after these boys? Because these Americanos aren't killers. These boys aren't anybody. They're as pure as the—you know—the rain or something."

"The driven snow," Costa says.

"You have no idea what you're doing," she says. "Do you."

"Maybe we already figured out that this is bigger than the Americanos. You may not be helping as much as you think."

"Sorry for wasting your time," she says.

"No need to apologize."

"I have information that could help. I followed this Heitor—I have pictures—"

"Go home, Luz. Keep yourself out of danger. Please."

"Take this." She puts a memory card in Costa's hand.

"Sure. Thank you very much."

"Don't patronize me."

"Do you have this Heitor's information?"

"Yes!"

"Write it down." Costa hands Luz a pad of paper.

"Those boys could be safe with their people right now. I still can't tell if you even grasp what is happening here."

"The Americanos are safe."

Luz leaves. She walks to the bus stop and waits. She rides south a couple of miles to the *Bompreço*, where she fills a cart with beans, rice, an onion, kitty litter, cat food, two industrial-size bottles of Pitú, several tubes of cookies, small white-paper packages of pork chops and ground beef, a green mango, and a bag of acerola berries.

She stands at the bus stop in front of the Bompreço. Her bus finally comes. She climbs the stairs, finds an empty seat, and sits with her heavy blue bag of groceries between her feet. The bus pulls away.

The bus stops and goes again. She looks up. She thinks she recognizes the man standing in the aisle above her. At the next stop, a seat opens up across the aisle to her left. He takes it. She gets a close-up look at the scar on his cheek. A perfect teardrop. She places him: the coconut man.

"Where are the elders?" he says.

"I don't know you. Where is who?"

"The elders," he says, quiet but sharp.

"You must think I am somebody else."

He laughs quietly. "You want a coconut?"

She is silent.

"You live next door to the Mormons," he says. "You have a cat. You drink. I've been watching you, and I don't like to see you paying visits to the Polícia Civil."

"You are a really clever guy. Congratulations. You managed to tail a broken-down old broad to the grocery store."

"Where are the elders?"

"They're gone. For good. North America. Have you heard of it?"

He casually looks out the window. "I don't believe you," he says. "Try again."

"That's all I know. They left in a hurry."

His hands grab the hems of his baggy shorts. He casually pulls them tight, revealing the distinct outline of a Glock deep in his right front pocket. He pats it gently.

"Where are they?" he says.

"I told you. Not very bright, are you?"

"This is our stop," he says.

He pulls the wire. The sign at the front of the bus lights up. As the bus pulls up to the curb, Luz jumps up. She drops her bag of groceries hard on his lap. She runs away from him down the aisle. She manages to put a few oblivious strangers between them.

"Excuse me," she screams, picking her way through people to the front of the bus. She hurries down the stairs and runs up the street.

The coconut man goes after her. "Senhora!" he shouts. "Senhora? Your groceries!" The door closes before he gets there. The bus pulls away from the curb. He puts his hand on the bus driver's shoulder. He points at Luz, now a block ahead of them. "That's my employer. She's having a hard time. The medication usually works better than this. She doesn't know any better, and I just don't want anything to happen to her. Do you mind?"

The driver gives him a tired, skeptical look.

"Come on," somebody shouts from the back of the bus. Other voices join in: "Help the man out. What's the big deal?"

The bus pulls up to Luz, who is no longer running. She carries her blue flip-flops in her left hand. She looks gassed. She doesn't seem to notice the bus—it doesn't stand out from all the others—until the door opens and the coconut man climbs down the stairs carrying her bag of groceries. He is completely calm. She runs into the only open door in sight, a plumbing supply store. He goes into the store after her. The bus pulls away.

He walks slowly up and down aisles of pipe and porcelain. The store is quiet. He listens for Luz as much as he looks for her. He makes his way around bathtubs and sinks and toilets. He eyes a door behind the counter at the back. It opens. A guy in white overalls comes out. He is bald and short. He has wide-set brown eyes and a plump, round nose. He perches himself on a stool behind the counter.

"How can I help you?" he says, not making eye contact.

"I lost something," the coconut man says. "What's behind that door?"

"You didn't lose anything back there, amigo."

The coconut man's hand plunges into the pocket with the gun in it. Then he sees something move out of the corner of his eye. He casually withdraws his hand. He goes that way, to a bin of scraps and odd pieces of PVC. White pipe with gray writing printed in a stripe down the side. He gives the bin a kick.

"Hey," the guy behind the counter says. "You got a problem, pal?"

He shoves the bin to one side. No longer hidden, Luz still cowers there in a ball on the floor.

"Senhora de Sá?" he asks. "Are you all right? You scared me. Come on. Let me help you up." He reaches down and pulls her up. He talks in her ear: "Wrong move, grandma. You can't make this go away. And you can't hide. I need to find the Mormons."

"Help!" she screams. "You!" she says to the guy in overalls. "Help me! This loser is trying to hurt me! He's got a gun!"

The guy in overalls eyes her nervously. His eyes jump from Luz to the coconut man and back to Luz. He is frozen by fear and uncertainty.

"This woman is very sick," the coconut man says. He is calm. "I care for her. She has these episodes. We were grocery shopping." He raises the blue sack. "And something just snapped. I just want to get her home. She needs her rest."

The guy behind the counter looks Luz up and down. "Need help, buddy?" he says to the coconut man. "You really can't tell who's crazy anymore just by looking."

"I'm not crazy!" Luz screams. "This man is a violent criminal!"

"She says the strangest things," the coconut man says with a forlorn smile. "You never know what will come out of her mouth next."

"He has a gun!" Luz screams. "Please, please don't let him take me."

"Now what would I want with a gun?" the coconut man laughs.

"There in his pocket!"

"Thanks for offering," the coconut man says. "Happens all the time. And you've got your business to look after. Come on, senhora." He puts his arm around Luz. "Let's go," he says. He leads Luz out of the store. "Sorry about this," he calls back to the guy behind the counter.

Now out on the sidewalk, he tightens his hold on Luz. "Let's take a walk," he says, leading her up the street. They take a left and keep walking, toward Ilha do Bicho.

The two of them walk well into the favela. He pushes Luz up a short alley. She stumbles and falls to the ground. He pulls out his gun and shows her the end of the barrel. "Last chance," he says. "Where are they?"

She sobs. "Will you leave me alone? I will tell you. Just promise."

"Sure. I promise."

"They are with the police. The Polícia Civil. They're holding the boys as suspects in a murder they obviously didn't commit. How don't you know this? That's why I went there. I went to see about the boys."

"Thank you," he says. He pulls the trigger three times. Three shots. Two in the chest. One in the head.

He turns away from her, stuffing his gun back in his shorts. He takes three steps before he sees someone standing between him and the open end of the alley. White hair. Sour, sunburned face. Awkward stance. The coconut man understands instantly. He reaches for his gun, but halfheartedly. "Severino," he says.

Severino puts two bullets in the coconut man's chest. Coldly. He forces a plastic sack of white powder into Luz's hand. He wipes his gun with a greasy handkerchief from his pocket. He puts Luz's prints on the gun and drops it by her side.

He glances from Luz to the coconut man and back to Luz. Just examining his work. He slowly limps away.

Chapter Fourteen

We are sprawled out on the floor in the interrogation room. Nordgren and I must look like we have been there for a while. Like we tried to sleep on the floor the night before and did not quite pull it off. We are tired and worried and cagey. It is the afternoon now, and Costa and Assis finally appear.

"Have you heard from our presidente?" I say.

"Yes," Assis says. "But nothing definite."

"We've been waiting all day! Holy fetch, guys!" Nordgren curses at them in Mormon. "We're going crazy in here."

"There is a flight late tonight. We hope you'll be on it."

"Hang in there guys," Costa says. "We have been busy. We were hoping we would have good news. More of it. Sooner."

"Your presidente still doesn't trust us. If we don't hear soon— we were thinking we would have you guys talk to him."

"Of course," Nordgren says.

Assis's phone rings. The ring tone is a Mamonas Assassinas

song. He answers. He listens for a minute, says yes twice, and hangs up. "Let's go," he says to Costa. "Ilha do Bicho. Two down. Maybe more. Some junkie apparently got herself shot by a traficante. Looks like she managed to return the favor too."

. . .

Costa and Assis drive to Ilha do Bicho. They find the alley, which is being watched by two patrol officers in dingy green uniforms. Costa stops at the feet of the first body, a tall black man in shorts and a T-shirt. He looks harmless except for the gun at his side. The two black holes in his chest are small. The cops approach the other body—all bronze arms and legs bursting out of a gaudy yellow sundress. They don't recognize her.

Costa goes down on one knee. Brushes hair away from her eyes. "Luz," he says.

"Luz," Assis says. "Damn."

Out of respect, Assis puts her ankles together and adjusts her dress so that it covers as much leg as possible.

They go back to the other body. Assis gets out the camera. He snaps pictures from various angles. "I can guess why they did her," he says. "But this guy—you don't think Luz actually—do you?"

"I don't."

"Everything about this is wrong. She didn't wander into this rat hole on her own."

"No. Sure."

Assis examines the blue plastic bag under the dead man's

arm. It is empty except for a receipt and the shards and smell of a shattered bottle of Pitú. "Booze," he says. He reads the receipt. "Bought this morning at the Bompreço. Not long after she left the station. Cookies. Meat. Fruit. Cat food."

"Cat food," Costa says.

"Why did he have her stuff?"

"Who knows."

"Where did it all go?"

"I'm sure it all found a good home. She made somebody's day with those groceries."

"Call the station," Costa says. "Gut feeling."

"What?"

"She left me some pictures. I asked somebody to make prints, which should be ready by now. Have them picked up."

• • •

The Cow Hand doesn't have a sign anymore. To people passing by, it is just a yellow door stained brown around the knob. From the street, you can see a faint rectangle on the wall above the door where the sign used to hang. There is one window, but somebody painted it black on the inside a long time ago. There is a short bar and some tables.

Brazilians call a cheap person a "cow hand" because a cow won't open its hand for anything. The Cow Hand never was a nice place, but it used to be a neighborhood hangout. Now it serves a particular type: lowlifes stalled somewhere in the middle of the criminal food chain. People you don't mess with mostly on account of their friends—the brains above them and the brutes below.

Costa and Assis go inside. They take two chairs next to a short guy with thin, greasy hair. He is drowning in a futebol jersey two sizes too big. It is gold with a green collar and a crest on the left side, the national team's colors.

"What's happening, Kaká?" Assis says.

"Cops," he says, "have a distinct odor."

"That's funny," Assis says. "I'm impressed. You don't look like such a sloppy drunk on TV. You play like one sometimes—"

The guy tells Assis to do something carnal to himself.

"Thanks for the tip," Assis says.

"I'm always good for that kind of advice."

"You really want to help, Emilio?" Costa says. "Take a look at this." He drops a picture on the table, the one Luz took of the guy with sunburn and the limp. "Have you seen this guy before? That three-story shack in the background is in Jardim Atlantica. Not far from here. Seems to be a happening place."

Emilio stares at the picture. He shakes his head no.

"Look again," Costa says. "Open your eyes this time."

"That pause wasn't pregnant enough?" Emilio says.

"Yeah. You saw something, didn't you? What?"

"A lot of nothing."

"*Besteira.*"

"Look, I couldn't recognize that face for all the girls waiting outside Kaká's locker room. Not for all the girls waiting outside all the locker rooms in Spain. Not for the all the girls—" He stops to finish his drink. "I could go on." He stands up.

"That's all right," Assis says. "Get your rest. Big game tomorrow, right?"

Emilio makes a fist. Then he lets it go. He stands up, cursing under his breath, and stumbles out of the Cow Hand. His head hangs down.

Costa and Assis pull up chairs next to two guys in the back corner. One of them is morbidly obese. The other one is sweaty and middle-aged and bald. Their table is a rough square painted yellow. The top is smeared brown by years of greasy food and hands. It groans under four sweaty arms, two glasses, and a large bottle of Pitú.

"Boa tarde," Costa says.

They just look at Costa and Assis. They smile.

"I said boa tarde. You forget your manners?"

"Drugs cause memory loss," the fat one says. His voice is high for such a big guy. And slow and irregular. Drunk voice. They laugh hysterically.

"Drugs cause something else too," the middle-aged one says. "What was it again?" More laughter.

Assis puts his hand on their bottle. He scrapes it across the table. They go quiet. "I suggest you listen," he says.

"If advice was worth anything, people wouldn't give it away," the fat one says. They erupt again in coarse laughter.

"Take a look at this picture," Costa says. "Tell me what you see."

The fat one drops a thick hand on the picture. "They say study is the light of life. That makes me something of an environmentalist."

"He don't study! Saves electricity! Get it?" the other guy says. More laughter—loud and stupid.

Costa lifts the thick hand from the table. The picture sticks to it. Costa peels it off. He holds it in front of them. "Have you seen this ugly mug before?"

"An ugly child has no father!" the fat guy says.

"It's true!" his friend erupts.

"Thanks for wasting our time," Assis says. "Thanks for the booze." He picks up the bottle.

"Don't steal," the other one says. "The government can't stand competition!"

The fat one slams both hands on the table. "They *are* the government!" he says. His voice is suddenly sharp. He stands up and jerks the bottle away from Assis. "Cops!" he says. He spits on the ground. Then he cracks up and falls back awkwardly into his chair. Pitú splashes all over his shirt. He laughs wildly.

Costa and Assis finally give up. They sit at the bar and order drinks.

They don't look at the other guy there. Costa just throws down the picture in front of him. "How scary is that?" he says.

"I'm too dumb to be scared," the guy says. He gets up.

"Sit down, Paulo," Costa says. "Don't make me say please."

"You don't know me, pig."

"Maybe this is my big chance. Let's chat."

"I was just leaving. I already forgot what you were saying anyway. I vaguely remember there was a picture involved. A picture of your mother, I think?" He points a thick finger at Assis. "Or was it his mother?"

"Or yours," Costa says. He grabs Paulo by the throat and jerks him back onto his barstool. Without releasing his grip, Costa slowly pours his drink into Paulo's lap. He moves close and tightens his grip. "You with these people? Talk. I mean it. *Talk.*"

"Get your little hands off me, cop. The only thing I have to do with this guy is not knowing who he is. And not walking on the same side of the street as him. And not breathing the same air."

Costa lets go of Paulo's neck. He returns to his stool next to Paulo. "Who in this place would know?"

"Nobody. Just—nobody. How would I know?"

"I've just got this feeling. Maybe I should tell people that Paulo sent me. I'll just say you said they would know all about this guy and his business."

"You wouldn't do that."

"I might. I mean, I don't know you. And I'm a pig. Isn't that right?"

"But—"

"Sometimes a cop just has to churn things up and see what floats. Strike a match and see what burns."

"But you know where I work. You know who I work for and what I do. I'm nobody! I put food on the table. I never use the junk myself. And I keep it away from the little kids if I can."

"How little?" Assis says.

Paulo shrugs.

"You're not helping yourself," Assis says.

"We just need to know," Costa says. "We can keep you out of it."

"Fine. Fine. Here goes nothing. Listen, we have our peace with these people. They don't move a lot drugs anymore, for one thing. They do their thing. We do ours."

"What are they into?"

"I don't know for sure. I have an idea."

"Well?"

"*Gente.*"

"Gente? As in people? Gente?"

"That's right."

"How does that work?"

"I don't know."

"What do you hear?"

"People talk about body parts packed on ice in coolers. Or they fly people to hospitals overseas. Take their organs and ship them back here. Apparently—sometimes—they just grab kids on the street."

"Nossa!" Assis says.

"This guy." He looks at the picture. "The ghost with the gimpy leg. His name is Severino. I think that's where he comes in. He grabs them. Moves them around. Buys and sells them. Ships them off to the States or wherever."

"This is common knowledge?"

"No. I don't know for sure. I mean, it's bad stuff. You hear things. This Severino is supposed to be some kind of sicko. I don't know. I keep my distance."

"What else do you hear?"

"Not much. People say there's all kinds of money in it. They say there's more cash in organs than drugs these days."

"Is it true?"

"I don't know. People don't get addicted to organs."

"I can't live without mine," Assis says.

Paulo groans.

"What else do you know?" Costa says.

"The main thing people say is"—his eyes sweep the room, and he leans in closer—"these are guys you just don't mess with. Tough. Connected. You know what I'm saying."

"Sure. For example, a guy got popped in the Opa this week," Costa says. "He was called Juvelino. You know who I'm talking about?"

"I didn't know that guy, but from what I heard, it figures."

"How so?"

"He handled money for them. They said he got creative with the cash flow."

"Who is in charge?"

"I've been talking to you guys way too long." He brings the palms of his hands together. He makes a praying gesture in Costa's general direction.

Costa ignores Paulo's plea for mercy. "Who?"

"The Elbow," he whispers.

"You can go," Costa says. He throws a few bills down on the bar and nods at the bartender.

The bartender grunts.

"Thanks for lending us your collection of punks," Costa says.

"Don't come back soon," the bartender says.

"We try to stay away," Costa says. "Your place is a blight on an already bad neighborhood. But it's very convenient for us."

...

"Worse than I thought," Costa says, driving back to the station.

"Gente," Assis says, amazed.

"The Elbow," Costa says with disgust.

"I know."

"We are moving them. I'm not screwing with the Elbow's machine."

"Right."

"They got to Luz. Chances are they know where the boys are."

"Right."

"Call the consulate. Call their president. Change of plans. Somebody needs to come pick them up."

Assis calls. He explains the situation, and he insists that they come and get the missionaries immediately. Says thank you twice and hangs up.

"Well?" Costa says.

"The consulate will send somebody. No promises about when. Something about too many fires and not enough water."

Chapter Fifteen

Costa and Assis are back in the interrogation room. Nordgren and I have been wearing the same clothes for two days now. We are bored and tired of waiting.

"Are we flying out of here?" Nordgren asks.

"Give us some good news," I say.

"We hope so," Assis says.

"We're not past *hope?*" I say. "What did our presidente say?"

"He left a message about a flight late tonight," Costa says. "Somebody is calling him right now about the details. Even before that—"

"Time for a change of scenery," Assis says. "I know you guys are going to miss this place."

"We are turning you two over to the Americano consulate," Costa says. "They are sending somebody up here to get you this afternoon."

"That *is* good news," Nordgren says.

"This is a precaution," Costa says. "That murder you witnessed—those people are organ traffickers. We didn't know that. We had them down as drug traffickers."

"What do you mean, *organ traffickers?*" Nordgren says.

"Some people ship in one piece," Assis says. "Some people—the lucky ones apparently—get auctioned off one kidney at a time."

"Does it matter what they traffic?" I say.

"Apparently they are real nasty," Costa says. "The other thing you should know—well, it's about your neighbor."

"Luz?" I say.

"She's dead," Costa says. He and Assis watch that news hit us.

"No," I say.

"Shot in an alley in Ilha do Bicho."

"Are you sure?" Nordgren says.

"We were just at the scene," Costa says. He puts his hand on my shoulder. "Don't be too hard on yourselves. It's not your fault."

"You mean it's not *my* fault?" I say. "Of course it isn't Nordgren's fault."

"It's not your fault, Elder Carson," Assis insists.

"You wouldn't say that if you weren't thinking it might be. And you are right. I dragged her into this."

"You didn't drag her," Nordgren says. "You didn't hurt her either. It was these organ traffickers."

"Luz was all grown up," Costa says. "She knew better. She never should have gone there. I mean, she staked them out. Took pictures and everything."

"She did?" I say.

"You are going to arrest them, right?" Nordgren says.

"Don't get your hopes up," Assis says.

"Why not?" Nordgren says.

"Let's assume we know these are the people who killed Luz," Assis says. "Let's say Luz *and* Juvelino. That doesn't make trying to arrest them our best move. It's not like they're going to stand trial."

"Why not?" Nordgren is incensed.

"Son," Costa says, "we don't have the firepower to fight an operation like this. We don't have the people. We don't have the politicians it would take to survive the aftermath."

"I can't believe this country," Nordgren says.

"Survival comes first," Costa says. "That's a fact. You've got to see things in context. This place is better today than it was ten years ago. If we get ourselves killed for nothing, who will take our place? Will they care about justice more or less than we do? Will the fact we got killed trying to do the right thing make the next guys more or less likely to do things like real cops?"

"So that's it?" I say. "What about Luz? And what about their victims?"

The door swings open. A cop pokes his head in. "Detective Costa," he says. "Call for you. I think you should take this."

Costa goes out. He comes back a few minutes later. He is different. Stiff. He won't look at me and Nordgren. "Assis," he says. "Call the consulate again. Call their presidente. They need to get them out of here *right now.*"

"What's going on?" Assis says.

"Call now," Costa says. "That was the Polícia Federal. They said they're interested in Juvelino—there's some kind of federal angle on it. I asked them what it was, and they told me to shut up."

"Just like that?" Assis says, already holding the phone to his ear.

"Yeah." Costa's distant gaze falls to the floor. "Some federal cops are on their way over here to talk to you boys. They're supposed to be nearby."

"I don't understand," I say.

"I am sorry," Costa says. "I told them you guys are clean. I said there was no need for further interrogation. I told them you were *absolutely clean* and we only held you here to keep you safe."

Silence.

"This guy said they might take you into custody," Costa says. "Somewhere else. I didn't like the way he said it. He was laughing, kind of. He said they've made arrangements to put you up somewhere nice and secure."

"What does he mean?" I say.

"Son," Costa says, "I am sorry."

"Probably the *Bruno Dos Rios*," Assis says. "Just a minute." He finishes his call. They wait. "They said they would make it a priority. Whatever that means."

"What's the Bruno Dos Rios?" Nordgren says.

"It's a prison in Recife," Assis says. "Calling it hell on earth would be an insult to hell. We didn't put you in our holding cell here because it is rough. We couldn't guarantee your safety. And there is no comparison between here and the Bruno Dos Rios."

"That's enough," Costa says.

"We can't just let them—" Assis says. "The Bruno Dos Rios?"

"What are we going to do?" Costa says. "Take on the Polícia Federal? I mean, it's one thing if we can turn the boys over to the Americanos. And even then—now that we know—that's sticking our necks out pretty far."

Someone pounds on the interrogation-room door. Two thick men come inside. They wear gray fatigues, black combat boots, and black berets. They have automatic rifles on straps over their shoulders. They strut up to the table.

"Get up!" one of them barks. He puts a finger on my chest. Then he turns to Nordgren. "You too. Get up!"

Nordgren and I stand up. They push us against a wall. They cuff us with our arms pulled behind our backs.

"Let's go," one of them says. "Move."

"Hold on," Costa says. "Officers. Good to meet you. Call me Detective Costa. You should feel free to use this room. We will help you out any way we can. You are here to interrogate them, right?"

"We have orders, detective."

"It's Costa."

"Be smart, Detective Costa. Don't get in our way."

"What orders?" Assis says. "From who?"

"These men are in federal custody now. You just ran out of authority."

"But—"

"Question-and-answer time just ended too."

"Hold on. That's not how I was briefed on the situation," Costa says. "This is my station, and these are my suspects."

Silence. The federal cops awkwardly twist me and Nordgren on our feet. They point us at the door. "Come on," one of them says. He pushes me in the back. "Move. Right out the door."

"This isn't the end of this," Costa says. "There is no federal angle. And you know it. I won't forget your faces!"

The federal cops don't seem impressed by Costa's speech. They lead me and Nordgren outside. They push us into the back of an old gray minivan. They cuff our ankles to the steel posts under the back bench. They turn on the siren and lights. We speed south toward Recife.

"Where are you taking us?" I say.

"Shut up," the cop in the driver's seat says.

"Prison," the cop in the passenger seat says. "You're going to love it."

They laugh.

"We have a right to call the United States consulate," Nordgren says. "We are United States citizens."

They laugh at that, too.

"You are going to regret messing with us," Nordgren adds.

Both cops glare at him in the rearview mirror.

We pass through the western outskirts of Recife. Mostly rough neighborhoods far inland from Recife's skyscrapers and beaches and cathedrals and ancient townhouses. The van passes a blur of dingy red-roofed buildings, graffiti, and lush green. We get stuck in traffic. The cop behind the wheel curses and honks the horn.

Nordgren points his chin at a bus to the side of us. I look. Two missionaries stand in the middle of the bus, each with an arm dangling from the overhead steel bar. It is dark now, and they are unmistakable in the well-lit bus: short hair, white short-sleeve shirts, ties, and black name tags. It is Elder Matos and Elder George.

I try to make eye contact with Matos. He and I were in the same district in the Casa Amarela zone four months earlier. I give Matos a look, urgent and wide-eyed. I mouth the word *help* over and over again. I nod at the cops in the front seat. Matos is unmoved. He doesn't recognize me or even acknowledge my panicked gestures. After a minute, he just looks away. Checks his watch. Smiles and says something—casually—to Elder George. Traffic starts to move, and we leave the bus behind.

We drive for a good hour. Then the van takes an abrupt right onto a dark road. We come to a gate in a tall concrete wall with three tiers of barbed wire across the top. A guard waves us through. The building is unimpressive, sterile, and ugly. Gray concrete stained in irregular blotches of black and green mold. No windows. Only vertical slits formed into the concrete.

The van pulls around behind the building and comes to a stop. The federal cops get out and go inside. They are gone for a long time. Finally they come back, smelling strongly of Pitú. They are with a prison guard who is being pulled by a snarling, drooling German shepherd. The prison guard's uniform is different, but he has the same black combat boots and automatic rifle on a strap over his shoulder. He wears a black helmet with a clear plastic shield over his face. He has expressive brown eyes and blue wings tattooed on the backs of both his hands.

The federal cops uncuff our ankles. Following the guard and the dog, they push me and Nordgren inside the prison. "All yours," one of them says, uncuffing our hands. "Send our regards to the big guy."

Chapter Sixteen

THE DOG SNIFFS AND BARKS and drools some more. The guard gives us an appraising look. He pulls on the dog's leash as he moves slowly backward to the door. He slams the door shut, locks it, and moves back toward us. The room is gray under a single dim light bulb.

The smell is overpowering, a mixture of disease, rancid food, sweat, urine, and feces. I fight my gag reflex unsuccessfully. Nordgren joins me. The guard just watches us retch. His face displays no emotion. The dog jumps and barks and laps at our vomit. We wait as the dog finishes its meal.

The guard puts his hand on his rifle. "Let's go," he says in English. His accent is thick. He opens a set of steel bars with an ancient key. We enter a dark corridor. We walk into the darkness. There is a steel grate maybe ten inches above our heads. We look up at the bottom of another guard's boots. He walks above us, rifle down at the ready.

There are steel bars—dark cells—on both sides of us. We can't see faces. But we hear what sounds like hundreds of voices as we pass cell after cell. Rats scatter as we approach, and now and then cockroaches crunch under foot. The smell grows worse the deeper inside the prison we go. It gets hotter too. The Bruno Dos Rios is a putrid sauna.

An arm reaches out of a cell and grabs a handful of my white shirt. The guard cracks the arm with the butt of his rifle. A voice attached to the arm cries, a loud burst trailing off into injured sobs. The guards keep walking and so do we.

Voices in the cells rise in response to the crying. The guard above screams for quiet. He clanks the business end of his rifle along the steel grate at his feet. Finally the guard below stops walking. The German shepherd growls and drools. The guard examines a ring of large keys under a flashlight.

"Get back," he screams into the cell. "Make room. Back! Back!" He opens the cell door. Its hinges grind and screech. The guard shoves me and Nordgren inside. He slams the cell shut, jerks on the bars once, and turns to go. The dog snarls. It lunges at the bars, leaps, and snaps its jaws inches behind our necks. The guard jerks on the leash. "Another day. Someday I'll feed them to you like cheap Americano sausages." The guard and his dog disappear back into the dim corridor.

Nordgren and I just stand there, backs to the bars. Slowly our eyes adjust to the darkness. The cell is about twelve by eight feet. There are four bunks and a black toilet on the back wall. I count the bodies. There are seventeen—nineteen with us. Like always, we are overdressed. None of them wears a shirt or shoes. Some sleep on the bunks. One makes his way to the toilet, drops his shorts, and squats. The rest lie side by side across the floor. Their faces—the ones that are awake—are set on us.

"Who are you?" one of them says.

We don't answer. We are frozen. Afraid.

"Who are you?" one of them screams. "Do you understand?"

"They don't speak Portuguese."

"Americanos."

"Rich *filhos de putas*."

"They understand everything. Look at their faces."

"Hey boys," one of them says. "I like white meat. Juicy and fresh. Do you understand? Get some sleep, because I'm going to eat you for breakfast."

Laughter. It fades into tense silence. Minutes pass. Nordgren and I are extremely tired. We sit down in the space created by the cell door swinging open.

I finally open my mouth—to cough violently. I swallow hard on the vomit still stuck in my throat. "Water," I say. "Do you have water?"

"What did I say? They understand—"

"No water."

"This isn't some beach resort, white bread."

"Tomorrow. We get water in the morning."

"Who are you?" one says. "Talk!"

One of them gets up. He steps over two sleeping bodies. He stops so close that he wedges his bare toes under Nordgren's crossed legs. He puts a hand under each of our chins, jerks our heads back, and examines our faces.

"Tell me one thing," he says. "What gang do you belong to?"

"We don't belong to a gang," I say.

"Everybody's in a gang."

"No," I say. "We are preachers. We are Christians."

"The Jesus gang," a voice says from the back of the cell.

Laughter.

"Everybody's in a gang. Our gang is the PCD. You are PCD soldiers now."

"No," Nordgren says. "We can't—"

"I'll talk slow so you understand, see? You are PCD or you are something else. If you are something else, I will kill you." His hand slides down Nordgren's neck. He squeezes with a sudden jerk. Nordgren is stunned. He gags and groans.

"Are you PCD? Or aren't you?"

"Stop," I say. "*Stop!*"

He doesn't. Nordgren's eyes start to roll back in his head. I think he is passing out. Then he manages to clock the guy hard on the ear. The guy's neck snaps sideways. They tumble awkwardly over sleeping bodies, wrestling and jabbing and gouging at each other. Nordgren gets free. He grasps at his own throat and gasps for air. The guy comes at him. Nordgren kicks him in the stomach.

Then something hard hits Nordgren in the back of the head. Out of the corner of my eye I see a thick hand gripping a piece of concrete the size of a softball. Nordgren slumps to the ground in a pile. A fat guy jumps on Nordgren's back. He cocks his arm to take another swing at Nordgren's skull with the concrete bludgeon. I lunge at him. I get my hands on it. Other guys pile onto me. I don't know how many. They are on top me, and I can't breathe.

"That's enough," a voice says from the top bunk on the right. He is sitting all alone on the edge of a bunk. "*Enough*," he says. His voice is firm and loud. The fighting stops.

"Get off," he says. "Both of them. Nobody touches the Americanos. Got it?"

The other prisoners nod. Some say, "Yes sir." The fat guy gets off Nordgren's back. He slaps Nordgren on the cheek, but soft. To wake him up. Nordgren opens his eyes. He is startled. He touches the back of his head, winces, and looks around. I give the fat guy kneeling over Nordgren a shove.

"Zezinho," the guy on the bunk says, "you watch the Americanos tonight. They will be—when I wake up—all in one piece." He lies back down on his bunk. He stares at the ceiling. "Now make some room. Let them stretch out. Come on. Move."

Zezinho stands barely over five feet tall. His arms and legs are thin, but he has a pot belly—round and hard. His glasses magnify his gentle brown eyes to a ridiculous size. He climbs over bodies and lies down between us.

"You guys all right?" Zezinho says.

"We're great," I say.

"That's funny," Zezinho laughs. "*Great!*"

"Yeah," I say. "This is just a dream come true for us. We would've stopped by sooner if only we'd known about this place."

"I like your style." Zezinho laughs. "It's all right to be afraid. I'd be worried about you if you weren't. You mixed it up well enough."

Silence. Minutes pass.

"And what about him?" Zezinho says. "Your friend—"

Nordgren softly touches the back of his head. He looks at the blood on his fingers.

"Concussion, I think," Zezinho says. "That rock made quite a pop when it hit your cranium, blondie. Did you hear it?"

Nordgren slowly nods his head yes.

"Anyway—try not to sleep, you know? Maybe you don't wake up again. You know what a concussion is?"

"Yeah," I say. "We get it."

Minutes pass. I watch Nordgren start to doze off. I reach across Zezinho and give Nordgren a shake.

"What is this place?" I say.

"They call it the *Casarão do Curado*. 'The Big House of the Cured One.' Proper name: Presidio Professor Bruno Dos Rios."

"The cured one," I say. "Sounds vaguely religious."

Zezinho laughs bitterly. "I don't know. I don't know what the disease was in the first place, and I certainly don't know who cured it. *Curado* is just the name of the neighborhood. This place has nothing to do with Jesus or Mary. I mean, look at you two. You said you're preachers. Look how far that got you."

"Right," I say.

"Anyway, you are PCD now," Zezinho says. "That's the important thing in this cell." He nods at the boss on the top right bunk. "Canudos is our *torre*. Torre. You understand?" he says slowly. "Means *tower*. He protects us and we protect each other. There is no other way. Only death. Understand?"

"I understand," I say.

"Most gangs start on the street. They are business first. Usually a drug business. They spread to prison one dealer at time. That's not the PCD. We started on the inside and worked our way out. We do business now on the outside. Drugs. Typical stuff. But the business arm of the PCD exists strictly to finance loftier goals."

I just listen. I give Nordgren another shake. He rolls over and groans.

"We are for human rights," Zezinho says. "Just look at this place. This cell is supposed to hold four men, tops. It's inhumane. All together, the Bruno Dos Rios is supposed to hold a thousand. And there are supposedly more than four thousand souls in this dump. So we help our families on the outside. Send ex-prisoners to college. Pay for lawyers. We fight for human dignity."

"Yes," I say. My voice is soft now. I am fading out.

"Most importantly"—Zezinho's voice rises—"we stage uprisings."

"Uprisings?" I ask.

"Riots. It's how we make certain demands," Zezinho says. "Nothing special, mind you. I'm taking about beds to sleep on. And clothes, and doctors, and edible food. You name it. This place is evil, my friend. You haven't seen anything yet."

"I believe you."

"You don't know the history of Brazil."

"That's true."

"The schoolbooks say the military dictatorship ended in 1985," Zezinho says. "But it still hasn't ended inside prison walls. The boss. The guards. They are sadistic. Do you understand me? *Sadistico?*" He says the word loud and very slowly. It hangs in the air above us.

I am too exhausted to react much. I just lie there, looking up at the ceiling.

"Wake up your friend," Zezinho says.

I give Nordgren a shake.

Zezinho pats his own belly thoughtfully. "I will tell you about dealing with the guards tomorrow," he says. "You've heard enough for tonight."

"All right," I say.

"Tell me something. What do you preach?"

"Like I said, we are Christians. But different. It's hard to explain."

"Try."

"For example, we have the Book of Mormon. It's like the Bible. I could probably get you one. Can you have books?"

"No books," Zezinho says. "I don't read much anyway. Just tell me something from the book. Hit me with your best homily."

"All right. I was just thinking about this story. There were two powerful teachers. Missionaries like me and Nordgren. They were preaching in a foreign country. Telling people to repent and believe in Jesus. And the people there didn't like what they heard. They threw the teachers in prison. They starved them. Stripped them naked. Tied them up. Judges and lawyers came to the prison to laugh in their faces and rough them up.

"Finally, one of the teachers prayed for strength. He said, 'Give us strength unto deliverance.' And they broke free. The judges and lawyers ran for their lives, but they didn't make it out of the prison before it collapsed. And they were crushed.

"People heard the crash, and they came running to see what

happened. This is what they saw: Their judges and lawyers were all gone, their prison was a pile of rubble, and these two teachers came walking out. So the people ran away. And I love this—it says they ran like goats running away from two young lions."

"That's good," Zezinho says. "Yes."

Minutes pass. Nordgren is sound asleep. I start to doze too.

"Do me a favor?" Zezinho says.

"What?" I say, suddenly wide awake.

"Give me a heads up if you guys decide to tear this place down, all right?"

I laugh quietly.

"It would be the ultimate uprising, no?"

I almost smile for the first time in days.

"I'm serious."

"All right. Yeah. Sure."

"Tonight?"

"No. You can rest easy tonight."

"Tomorrow?"

"Maybe."

"It's hopeless keeping your friend awake."

"I know," I say. "Me too."

Chapter Seventeen

I AM ASLEEP. I don't remember the night before or the Bruno Dos Rios. I don't even remember Brazil. There is a chopping sound. I dream of a tree back home. A broad blue spruce that towers over the little square house across the street from my childhood home. Every year on the day after Thanksgiving, my neighbors rented a crane to hang strings of lights on the tree. The old-fashioned kind with the big glass bulbs. Red, yellow, blue, and green. I dream of an ax. More chopping.

I roll over and open my eyes. Nordgren lies there still sound asleep. Zezinho stands above him, a chunk of concrete in his hand. The same one from last night. It drips red. I look down at Nordgren again. There is a body sprawled out next to him—the guy who started the fight last night. His face is smashed awkwardly into the floor, and the side of his head doesn't look right.

"Fernando tried to mess with your friend again," Zezinho

says. His voice is soft. "Your pal here was still out cold. Look at him! He tried to rape him."

"Is my friend all right?"

"Nothing happened." He pats himself on the chest. There are little specks of blood on the back of his hand. "He doesn't even know. I took care of him. Both of you—I took care of both of you."

I look at the body. I start to vomit, but there is nothing there for my stomach to reject. I want to look away from the body, but somehow I can't. I get up. Disgusted and amazed and grateful, I look back at Zezinho.

"What? Don't give me that look. Did I have a choice? It was him or your amigo."

Nordgren stretches and scratches his neck. He rolls over, and his hand falls on the dead man's back. I move Nordgren's hand. I decide that isn't good enough, so I carefully pull Nordgren away from the body. The other prisoners ignore us and the body. They are quiet. Somber. Sunlight gradually fills the cell, filtering in through irregular holes in the ceiling. The cell grows even hotter than before.

After an hour or so, a guard comes to the cell door. "Man down," Canudos says from his bunk. "May need medical attention."

"Sure," the guard says. "Whatever you say, Canudos. A doctor might stop by the prison any week now." The guard's thick laughter stops abruptly when he sees the body. "Oh, come on!" he whines. "Who did this?"

"He slipped and hit his head," Canudos says. "Never mind about the doctor. This guy stinks. We want him out."

"*Besteira*, Canudos. You know the drill. You have one hour to give me the name of who did this. Then I tell *you* who is responsible. You won't like who I choose."

"He slipped," Canudos says.

"Somebody pays," the guard says.

"Ask any man in this cell," Canudos says.

The guard looks at me. I look at my feet.

"Talk, Americano. Which one of these animals busted his head in? I know you speak the language. Let's have it."

I shrug like I don't understand. I'm as silent as the dead man on the floor. I look at Nordgren, who still sleeps face down.

"One hour," the guard says. He hacks at something in his throat and spits on the rough concrete floor. "Somebody pays! Until then, your former friend here stays put. Maybe the stink will jog your memory."

The guard leaves. Soon another guard comes. He only shrugs at the body. He passes out small foil dishes of breakfast. Cold beans and rice. Gritty. Bland. Undercooked. He also passes out sulfur-flavored water in greasy unwashed tin cups. The guard offers to sell us other stuff too. Things he brought in from the outside. He has a bag of oranges over one shoulder and a bag of stale rolls on the other. There are no takers. The guard and the other prisoners all look at me and Nordgren.

"We don't have any money, guys," I say. The guard leaves.

Canudos climbs down from his bunk. He sits down between me and Nordgren. "Big day, right?" he says.

"Uprising?" I say.

Canudos laughs. "You never know," he says. "It has been a while."

"Yeah?"

"I'm talking about you. It's no use playing dumb with me. The word is you guys are here to see the Elbow."

"The Elbow?" I say. "Is that a person?"

"Sure," Canudos says. "Play it cool."

"Play what cool?" I say.

"So I'm supposed to believe you don't know about Fausto Gomes—also known as the Elbow—the most powerful man in northeastern Brazil?"

"Even if we knew about him, how would he know anything about us?"

"He had you brought here."

"Why?"

"That's what I want to know."

I look at Nordgren, still sleeping peacefully. I am speechless. After a good pause, I break the silence. "Why do they call him the Elbow?"

"I don't know," Canudos says. "I never had the chance to ask him."

"We don't have anything to do with him," I say.

"You can tell me the truth. For example," Canudos says, "tell me you guys are trying to muscle in on him. Is that it? Because I need a good laugh."

Nordgren rolls over and opens his eyes. "Maybe the Elbow wants to talk religion," he says. "Maybe *he* understands that we are just missionaries. There is no other reason to talk to us."

"I can't believe I like you guys." Canudos laughs. "No, I don't think that's it."

"Why not?"

"The Elbow is a famous Spiritualist," Canudos says. "They say he makes contact with the souls of all the dead he has left in his path."

"We have been in trouble," I say. "Obviously. We are here. But I have no idea how the Elbow comes into it."

"I don't either," Canudos says.

Minutes later, a guard comes to the cell. "Let's go, Americanos," he says.

"Take care of yourselves," Canudos says.

"Where are we going?" Nordgren asks.

"Shut up," the guard says.

"That's what I love about this place," Nordgren says to me in English. "The customer service."

The guard takes us on a long walk deeper into the prison. Eventually the smell of tobacco hits us. It is overwhelmingly sweet compared to the predominant stench of the Bruno Dos Rios. I inhale it with relish. Nordgren whistles. The guard stops short. He nods at a cell door. It is wide open. We go inside.

Four men sit at a table playing poker and smoking huge cigars with ornate gold foil bands on them. Four brown bottles of beer sweat on the table. The flat-screen TV on the wall behind them—the sound turned way down—plays a futebol match. There are two refrigerators. The cell is dominated by a tall king-size bed. The bedspread is lustrous purple and gold satin, quilted in a fleur-de-lis pattern. There are easily twenty pillows on the bed, arranged in a neat formation. Lots of garish gold fringe and tassels. I'm amazed by the odd juxtaposition of moldy concrete and gaudy luxury. The difference between this cell and the rest of the Bruno Dos Rios.

It is not hard to guess which one of the men at the table is the Elbow. He is fat. About five feet ten inches. He wears baggy gold linen pants, leather sandals, and a billowing black linen shirt. The top two buttons of his shirt are undone, exposing a fine gold chain and a few long, thin wisps of black chest hair. A plush black nest of hair climbs up his back, onto his head, and stops a few inches short of his forehead. His fingers are stubby and fat and vaguely grotesque.

The man seated across from the Elbow has a long sunburned face underneath a shock of stark white hair. He is stiff, uneasy. The other two men are short and black. They could be brothers—they have the same squatty build and the same bug eyes.

The Elbow's cell phone rings. He checks who is calling with a grim, irritated face. He slams down his cards and answers. "What?" he says. "I'm busy." He gets up from the poker table talking loud and fast, jabbing the air with his well-chewed cigar. He finally notices us. He gives us half a smirk each. He excuses the guard with a contemptuous flicking gesture, like the guard was a fly that just tried to land on his steak dinner. The guard doesn't make eye contact with the Elbow or the other men. He just backs away, eyes fixed on his boots.

Something clicks on the back wall. An air conditioner. It cranks up, pumping air into the cell so cold that a chill comes over me. We wait, watching the Elbow hate the person on the phone with his deep voice, his round face, and his crude fat hands.

The Elbow ends his call. "Welcome to my office, boys. They really should not try to put a certain kind of guy in a cage, you know? This is how it turns out. Ridiculous! Trust me, I know." He pats his stomach. He scratches it. "I own this place. Every disgusting centimeter. The guards around here don't breathe without my permission. Ask anybody."

We don't say anything.

"Beer?" the Elbow says.

"No thanks," I say.

"Nonsense," the Elbow says. "Two beers," he barks in the general direction of table. One of the black guys at the table drops his cards and goes to the fridge.

"Save it," Nordgren says. "We don't drink."

The Elbow gives us a vicious look. His crony pops the caps off two beers and forces them into our hands.

"You drink if I say so," the Elbow says. "This is called hospitality. You take what you can get around here. Don't you know what today is? It's carnaval! So drink up. I don't care if you enjoy it. Show some respect for our traditions."

We don't say anything. We don't drink, either. We just stare at the Elbow.

"Apparently you prefer acid rain collected in barrels off the roof. I could get some of that for you. Isn't that right, boys?"

The guys around the table agree in grunts and dumb laughter. They are shifty but weak. Completely cowed by the Elbow.

We hold the cold brown bottles at our sides. We clutch them carefully, like they might explode.

Chapter Eighteen

"I don't like Americanos," the Elbow says. "I never have. Except for Charlie Chaplin. And Michael Jackson."

"Marilyn Monroe," a guy at the table says.

"Elvis," another one says.

"Other than them," the Elbow says. He raises a hand to make them stop. "They're all dead anyway." He laughs. "Dead Americanos, I don't mind. And you two. I mean, just look at you. *Caramba!* What can I do?" He laughs again, slow and deep. His men laugh on cue.

"I need some answers. Understand? You talk, and who knows, maybe things won't be so bad for you."

"We'll tell you what we can," I say.

"Who are you?" the Elbow says.

"We're Mormons," I say.

"Who do you work for?"

"Do you mean our church?" I say.

"I mean, why are you doing this to me? Why now? What do you want?"

Nordgren and I look at each other. We are confused.

"We are nobody, as far as you are concerned," I say. "We don't want anything to do with you. We don't want any trouble."

"No. Wrong. Too late. Elder Carson saw two of my guys shoot some old loser. That's you"—he points at me. "Fine. There are always bullets flying around. One of those guys doing the shooting happens to be my kid. The other one—Heitor—is a favorite of mine. My kid's a complete screwup. And it's my fault, too. I work hard to make things easy for him, and the kid has no idea what it takes. He's a dumb little pussy cat.

"But this Heitor kid. Nossa! He has brains. He's tough. Rocks. Nails. Whatever. I don't mean just with a gun in his hand, either. I like to say he's exactly like me at that age. Kid has a future with me. But something bothers me. I think he saw you at the Opa that night. I think he saw you—and he just let you walk away. So I asked him about it, and he said no. Did he lie to my face? I don't know.

"And the next thing we know some old broad—your next-door neighbor—is staking us out. And she's taking pictures and talking to cops. And what else can we do? She has to go. Things like this put my family in danger. My whole business! Everything!

"So now you get yourself picked up by the cops. And apparently the Americano Embassy is calling everybody in the phone book. And senators. Newspapers. Amnesty International. They tell me your faces will be on the cable news soon. You will be famous! This is obviously a problem."

"I haven't talked to anybody," I say. "I don't know anything. These cops—they wouldn't leave us alone."

Silence. The Elbow approaches the bed. He goes down on his knees and reaches for something underneath. He pulls out a pistol. It is big and square.

"We just want to disappear," Nordgren says. "We'll leave Brazil today. We don't want to bother you!"

"It's not our fault," I say.

"It's a special edition." The Elbow admires the gun. "Notice the rosewood." He shows us the grip. "And the gold accents. Made in Brazil. Of course, it's a remake of a famous Italian gun. Maybe you have seen the boring version of the same thing before—it happens to be the official sidearm of the Americano army. Anyway, my problem is this: you are supposed to be good people. That means I can't just let you walk out of here. I can't take your word for it that you won't cause me any trouble."

"We came to your country to teach people about Jesus," Nordgren says. "That's all. We have families. We don't want to get mixed up in your business. We just want to go home."

"That's what they told me you would say. *Missionaries*. My business is—let's face it—it's very misunderstood. I can't trust anybody. I have to bribe everybody. Or kill them. I mean—if you somehow got out of this, you would have to do something, right? Because we are talking about children! And I know how it goes. It is better to be drowned in the ocean with—what is it again?—a millstone strapped to your neck. No matter what you say, I know you would love to hang a big rock around my neck."

We don't deny it.

"I've been thinking about this," the Elbow says. "We were just going to let you take the fall for the murder charge. What was his name?"

"Juvelino," Nordgren says.

"Right. Justice can be swift under the right circumstances. A discreet little trial. A quick execution."

"Fine," I say. "A trial. Fine."

"It's not fine anymore," he says. "People all over the world are going to know who you are. Questions will be raised. People will have certain expectations. No. No. No. I would rather have you die in jail before a trial ever happens. Officially speaking, you are still in Olinda where we found you. People die in jails every day. It's just what happens. Your family will make sense of that. The other Mormons. The people all over watching the news. A tragic coincidence just makes sense to people. It's not so personal."

"Please just let us go," Nordgren says. "We only want to forget about all this."

"I'm not finished," the Elbow says. "There is also a plan C. Why? Because I am a business man. And plan B seems like such an awful waste. I have looked you over. You seem healthy. Have either of you had any serious diseases?"

"I had dengue fever a few weeks ago," Nordgren says.

"What strain? Do you know?" the Elbow says.

"It was nasty. My joints swelled up and I had a fever and I couldn't walk five steps without getting dizzy and almost falling down."

"And yet today you are feeling much better, am I right? You are healthy boys!"

"I'm feeling great." Nordgren stares the Elbow down.

"It doesn't matter anyway. We can actually cure diseases in the organs themselves post operation. It's amazing, actually."

"What's plan C?" Nordgren asks.

"We send you to a private hospital. It is close. I'm one of their biggest shareholders."

I can feel Nordgren shaking next to me. My heart pounds in my ears so loud I can barely hear. I start to say something—to plead for my life—but I stop short.

The Elbow shrugs. "I have always liked the word *harvest*, you know? It seems so peaceful when you put it like that. It is harvest time. Throw a big party. Pass the sweet corn. Harvest time. Anyway—let me finish now that you got me started—what's left of you guys after the hospital comes back here. Maybe you get lucky and die in a prison riot. More likely, the bacteria gets you. This is no place to recover from major surgery."

Chapter Nineteen

"Kidneys, livers, eyes, and skin," the Elbow says. "These are my bread and butter. There was a time when it was basically family organs or nothing, you know? There's no market in that. Have a seat." He points at the bed.

Nordgren and I sit on the edge of the Elbow's bed. The futebol game on the TV is over. The Elbow hands the Brazilian Beretta with the rosewood grip to the guy with the sunburned face and the white hair. He watches us machinelike, no interest or emotion.

The Elbow and the other two watch a parade. The floats are elaborate, more colorful than macaws. Thousands samba on and around them. Their garish costumes cover very little flesh. Torsos and breasts and thighs—slathered in oil and dusted with glitter—shimmy and gyrate down a road enclosed by stadium seats. They twirl umbrellas and pinwheels and giant leaves and feathers of every unnatural color. There are fireworks too.

Carnaval broadcasting live from the *Sambadromo* in Rio de Janeiro.

We don't watch the parade, at least not with any pleasure. Our hearts are pounding. We are both praying silently for deliverance.

"Do you realize what kind of advances have been made in antirejection drugs in the past ten years?" the Elbow says to us over his shoulder. "These things are absolutely amazing. Just amazing. I probably have Americanos to thank for that. That and the *Thriller* album." He laughs at his own joke. "They have certainly made me a good hunk of *masa*. You should see the trends, amigos! My little business has grown every quarter for three years. It is a beautiful thing."

We don't stop praying. We ignore him.

"Are you really going to waste those beers?" the Elbow says, still not looking at us over his shoulder. "That is a crying shame. You know, hundreds of men in this place—no, thousands—would do absolutely terrible things to you just to lay their hands on those bottles of suds." The Elbow chews and puffs at his cigar. "Where is that guard, anyway? These government employees are ridiculous. He's probably taking a nap in a hammock somewhere."

"Please don't do this," I say. "Please. We have families. We just want to go home. We promise! We'll never say or do anything that could possibly hurt you." My voice trails off. Nordgren picks up where I left off. Pleading for our lives. The Elbow and his men are completely entertained by the parade. They ignore us.

"Repent," I finally say.

"What?" the Elbow asks.

"Repent!" I give it to him louder. I figure we are dead anyway. And that we may as well do what we were called to do. "Tremble and repent of your sins!" I have their attention now—the Elbow and his men all have their eyes fixed on me. "That is the last thing we are going to say to you. You think you are on top of the world. You are lost! Look around you. I don't care how soft your bed is—this is hell! And now is the time to repent. It may not be too late. But if you do this to us—I am telling you—God will be your judge. Our blood will cry for vengeance, and God will hear those cries. I don't know how or when, but I promise you it will happen. Things much worse than what you could ever possibly do to us."

They are still looking at us, their faces inscrutable. I think I have made an impression. Then they burst into laughter. All four of them in unison.

"Forget it," Nordgren says. "They are past feeling."

A prison guard finally appears. The Elbow gives him instructions. He draws the guard a map to the hospital. "The doctor is waiting," the Elbow says. "He doesn't like to wait. It gets very expensive for me, understand?" He puts a fat finger in the guy's face. "Get them out of here! Now!" He turns to the guy with the sunburn and white hair. "Severino," he says. "Show them to their car."

The guard pulls me and Nordgren off the bed. He cuffs us, arms behind our backs, and shoves us toward the cell door. Severino follows us with his wild, grinding limp. He keeps the gun on us. The four of us walk back down the same dank prison corridors. The prison stench fills our mouths and noses, and cockroaches once again crackle under our feet. This time the walk through the prison doesn't seem long enough.

"Don't worry," Severino says. "We'll find good hosts for your organs. We'll get top dollar for them, guaranteed."

"Shut up, freak," Nordgren says.

"What's that?" Severino says. "What?" He jabs the gun into Nordgren's back.

"What are you going to do?" Nordgren says. "You going to shoot me? Go ahead! There won't be any surgery if you pull that trigger. And I'm good with that. Personally, I prefer getting shot."

"Oh yeah?"

"Do it! Come on! Shoot me!"

Severino laughs. "How about this? I'll gladly shoot you after the doctors harvest your organs. Is that fair? I'll be here waiting for you. You won't see me, of course, because they are going to take your pretty blue eyes. But I will be seeing you."

The afternoon is humid and hot and blindingly bright. The fresh air burns in our noses and lungs. The guard walks us to a white van. The flag of the state of Pernambuco is painted on the sides and back. The top half of the flag is royal blue with a gold star above a rainbow above a stylized gold sunburst. The bottom half of the flag is a red cross on a white field. The driver slides open the side door and forces us inside. Unlike our prior guards, he doesn't cuff our ankles to bars under the bench. I don't know why. He walks around the van, climbs into the driver's seat, and studies the Elbow's hand-drawn map to the hospital.

Severino stands to the side of the van watching. His white hair glows in the sunlight. His sunburned face seems to have taken on a darker shade of red. He taps on the passenger-side front window with the round steel end of the fancy knock-off Beretta. "What's taking so long? You stupid or something? The doctor is waiting!"

The guard turns the key in the ignition and grinds the stick shift into gear. The van jerks forward. Severino watches us pull away. Nordgren and I look back at him as we go. Severino points the gun directly at Nordgren. He gives Nordgren a wink and makes like he is firing the gun.

The guard drives through the gate and pulls onto the highway. Traffic is heavy.

"Where are you taking us?" Nordgren asks.

"You know," he says.

"The hospital. Is it far?"

"No."

We come to a red light. It is a busy intersection. I get up. Nordgren follows me. We slowly advance from the back seat toward the driver. Without slowing down, the guard pulls over onto the shoulder to go around the traffic stopped at the light. He hardly taps the brakes at the intersection. His head jerks left, right, and left again. He floors it. The tires squeal, and the van lurches into the intersection. That's when the guard looks in the rearview mirror, and he finally sees us coming.

"Sit down," he screams.

We ignore him.

"Get back!" he says, reaching for us with his right hand. He punches wildly. Grasps at nothing. His right hand returns briefly to the front seat. It comes back attached to a gun. We are far enough behind him that he can't quite point it at us. He fires it anyway. The back window shatters.

"Please shoot us," Nordgren says. "I really hate hospitals."

The guard drops the gun on the passenger seat. He grasps the steering wheel with both hands and hits the gas hard. Nordgren and I are tossed backward. Nordgren hits the ground in front of the back bench, and I hit Nordgren. Slowly, hands still cuffed behind our backs, we fight to get up again and advance once more.

The guard swerves violently. We are tossed hard against the driver's side of the van between the back benches. I hit my head on something: a chrome window opener, the old-fashioned crank kind. I feel warmth, my own blood, pour slowly over my left temple and down my jaw. We stagger back to our feet, and the guard swerves sharply in the opposite direction. We are tossed hard against the passenger-side sliding door. Again, we fight desperately to regain our feet. The van approaches another intersection. Another red light. The guard is forced to slam on the brakes. We are tossed forward like a couple of rag dolls. Nordgren throws himself against the back of the front passenger seat and somehow remains upright. I slam into Nordgren.

The guard slowly steers the van out onto a narrow shoulder above a steep drop-off. He looks left, then right. Nordgren reels sideways toward the guard. He falls forward and head butts him in the ear. The van veers right. I am thrown into the guard. I hit him hard with my forehead at the base of his skull. I almost black out. The van veers left. Nordgren goes again; this time the guard's head slumps forward.

The van rolls into the intersection. A red hatchback on our left slams into our driver's-side rear fender. The van spins. We are tossed once more sideways against the passenger-side sliding door. The van hits the curb after a few revolutions. It stops suddenly, almost tipping over onto the sidewalk. We stagger once more to our feet.

The guard expels a pained groan from deep inside his throat. His head has shattered the driver's-side window. Little chunks of glass are everywhere. He is slumped to the side, the weight of his upper body hung over the shoulder belt. His face is broken up, and blood gushes out of his left ear. He groans again.

Smoke pours out of the van's engine. The hatchback behind us is in flames, and we can't see any signs of life. Traffic moves around us. It slows down only slightly as drivers steal fleeting glances at the wreckage. I turn my back to the sliding door and let my cuff-restrained hands fumble awkwardly with the handle. It finally budges after countless tries. We run up the street and duck into a shop called the Little Egyptian, a dump with bars on the windows. It is full of beer, cigarettes, and dirty magazines.

"You got a phone?" I say.

"No," the old man behind the counter says. He is marking the handcuffs and the blood running down the side of my head.

"You have to help us," Nordgren says. "You don't have a cell?"

"We're closed," he says, reaching for an overhead metal screen between him and us. He slams it down and locks it into place.

"Please," I say. "This is an emergency!"

The old man sinks down behind the counter. "I'm calling the police now!" he says.

"Good," I say. "That's who we need. Can you call a particular station for us? We need Detective Costa. He's in Olinda."

"Costa?" he says. "Olinda?"

"That's right," I say.

"You got a number?"

"We don't. Can you find it?"

"I'll try."

"Just tell him we are here," I say. "He'll know what that means."

"You should call the local cops too," Nordgren says. "There has been an accident. Just here in front. Both drivers—they might still be alive."

"I'm locking up," I say. With my back to the window, I make my cuff-restrained hands turn the sign to *Closed*. I even manage to hit the light switch with my chin. I can hear the man behind the counter dialing. He talks to someone. I hear the word *Costa* once and the word *Americanos* twice. He goes quiet.

"Well?" I say.

"They are coming. I'm calling on the accident now. Somebody—I don't know—somebody is coming."

Eventually an old blue Fiat pulls in front of the store. Assis jumps out of the car and pounds on the door. We go with him. Assis hits the gas and swerves into traffic. We leave the smoking totaled cars behind us.

"You guys all right?" he says.

"We're fine," I say.

"You look terrible."

"Thank you." I get choked up, I'm so happy and relieved. "I mean it, man. Thank you for coming for us."

Assis is quiet. Driving fast. Nervously checking his mirrors.

"Where is Costa?" Nordgren says.

"He couldn't make it."

"I didn't know if we would see you again," I say.

"I know," he says. "I didn't think I—that you—" He doesn't finish his thought.

"Where are we going?"

"The airport."

"So we have a plane to catch?" I say.

"I hope so."

"What do you mean?" I say.

"I'm going to leave you at the airport. Your people are making arrangements. I've got a phone card here for you. You're going to call your presidente when you get there. That's all I know—"

"We saw him," I say. "The Elbow. We were just in his cell. We were sitting on the Elbow's bed talking to him. You know about the Elbow, don't you?"

"People say he lives pretty good in prison," Assis says. "There isn't a cop in northeastern Brazil who doesn't know about the Elbow. They say he has wild parties in there. Women and drugs and everything."

"That place was miserable," I say. "Awful. There are no words. They stuck us in a little cage with about twenty other guys. And the Elbow down the hall lives like a king. His cell door was wide open. He was actually ordering the guards around. And he's got guns and beer and an air conditioner and a flat screen mounted on the wall."

"We didn't see any women," Nordgren says.

"People say he still runs things on the outside," Assis says.

"He had a phone," Nordgren says. "And he was ordering people around with it. And he kept bragging to us about his business—"

"What's going to happen to the Elbow?" I say. "Can you guys stop him?"

"He is already locked up," Assis says. "Serving a life sentence, if I remember it right. You saw what that was like with your own eyes. He's safe from his rivals in there, and the organ business is good. That isn't enough justice for you?"

"What about the others? The kidnappers? The doctors?" Nordgren says.

"It's tough," Assis says.

"What about the murderers?" I say. "What about Luz and Juvelino? Do their lives mean anything?"

"They don't," Nordgren says. "Don't forget the survival speech. It comes first. And you guys are much better people than whoever might replace you. It was a good speech."

"We built a case over the last few days," Assis says. "We have pictures and statements. Other cops—friends of mine—have talked to people who sold organs to the Elbow. Poor people. Junkies. And mothers and fathers who had their babies taken and were too weak to do anything about it. We have stuffed a file with names and faces, and we turned it over to the federal cops. And not these creeps who took you. It found the hands of some good people."

"Why don't you do it?" I say.

"You don't get it," Assis says. "We are through. This thing is too big, and we hung ourselves out there too far. Costa got on a bus to São Paulo with his wife and kids yesterday. My fiancée and I are leaving to Mato Groso do Sul tonight."

"We didn't know," I say.

"We won't be back," Assis says. "We could be dead. We certainly aren't going to push our luck with the Elbow."

"Thank you again," I say.

"Don't," Assis says. "Because it isn't enough. Even if they take down the biggest organ-trafficking ring in northeastern Brazil. Chances are three more groups pop up to take its place. And maybe they are worse. Greedier. More bloodthirsty. At war with each other. It has happened before."

Chapter Twenty

ASSIS REMOVES OUR CUFFS in the airport parking lot. He cleans the blood off the side of my head with some napkins out of his glove box. It is crowded inside. Following closely behind Assis, we shove our way through travelers coming and going. We come to a tiny cafe. Assis hurries us past empty tables, through a swinging door, and into a greasy little kitchen.

"Where's Paulinho?" Assis says.

"He was just here." The cook gives us a tired look. "You the guys?"

"Yeah," says Assis.

The cook shrugs. "He'll be back."

"Wait here." Assis slaps me gently across the back. "I don't have all day."

The cook offers us coffee no less than seven times before throwing in the towel. After about ten minutes, Assis comes back with a short, thick guy with heavy black eyebrows and a matching mustache. The silver name tag that holds his burgundy tie to his sweat-soaked shirt reads "Paulo R."

"Paulinho will get you through security," Assis says. "He's OK. You have the phone card? Call your presidente. And just lay low. Don't call attention to yourselves. Don't sit in one spot for too long."

"Thanks again, Assis," I say.

"Good luck," Nordgren says. We hold out our hands. He shakes them.

"You guys are too nice," he says. "Go home. Please. *Vão com Deus*. I sincerely hope I never see you guys again."

Paulinho doesn't take us through security. Instead, he opens an unmarked door outside the metal detectors with a white card on his key chain. He leads us down a long hallway. Easily beyond the security checkpoint. He stops in front of a door at the end of the hallway and opens it about three inches. He scans cautiously from left to right. He opens the door and stands back to let us through.

"Go on," he says. "If you have trouble—please understand—I have never seen you guys before. Don't ask for me. Don't say my name."

"We won't," I say.

"We promise," Nordgren says.

Paulinho's eyes give the terminal another nervous once-over. "Quick," he says. "Walk away and don't look back."

We go.

"We're going home," Nordgren says.

"I'm not relaxing until our feet touch American soil.

Especially your feet, dude. On the sand somewhere in San Diego."

"Can you imagine telling people back home about all this?"

"No."

"Would they even believe us?"

"*I* don't believe it," I say, staring absently out the window at a big commercial jet taxiing from the runway to the terminal.

"I'm freaking tired," Nordgren says. "Have we gone far enough?"

"A little farther," I say. "Let's turn this corner, and we'll stop at the first phone."

"I'm going to sleep for a week when I get home," Nordgren says. "And kiss girls. I don't how many. But girls will be kissed."

"You deserve it, dude."

"So do the girls. Whoever they may be."

"Of course."

"And the homecoming talk," he says. "I almost forgot about that! I'm not sure how you work the past few days into a homecoming talk."

"Best homecoming ever," I say.

"Brothers and sisters, I would be ungrateful if I did not stand before you today at this pulpit and acknowledge that the last three days of my mission were the best two years of my life."

We come to a phone. I make the call. Presidente Ford picks up.

"Elder Carson?" he says. His voice is all relief and anxiety.

"Yes, presidente," I say.

"Is Elder Nordgren with you?"

"Yes."

"Are you all right?"

"Yes."

"And Elder Nordgren?"

"Fine."

"You're at the airport?"

"Yes."

"We have you on a flight leaving at—what is it?—11:20 tonight. That is actually plan B. Long before then, a small jet is going to land there to refuel. A member of the church makes his jet available on an emergency basis. We need to get you down on the tarmac. I don't know if it will be by a gate. They tell me there are only eleven gates total. You are looking for a white Gulfstream. A small jet. There will be a man under the nose of the plane pretending to fix something. Got it?"

"Yes, Presidente."

"Call me if you don't get on the jet. In that case—I will personally deliver your passports and tickets for the other flight."

"*Obrigado*," I say.

"You guys are going to be all right."

"Presidente?"

"Yes, Elder Carson."

"I almost forgot. We have two young couples committed to be baptized. One of them has to get married first. Can you send somebody to follow up with them?"

"Of course."

"You want their information? I don't have exact addresses. I can get you close."

"Later, Elder Carson. There will be time for that. We'll talk again soon."

Chapter Twenty-One

We walk through the terminal. We try to act natural while scanning the tarmac for the jet. We walk to the end of the terminal and all the way back. We don't see anything close to the jet Presidente Ford described. We sit down and act like we are waiting to board a plane with everybody else.

I start to doze off after a while. I am startled awake by the sound of Nordgren's voice. Sharp but not loud. "Shit," he says.

"What?"

"Don't look."

I look over my shoulder but only for a second.

"Careful," he says.

"Him," I say.

"What do we do?" Nordgren says.

I glance at him again over my shoulder. White hair. Face sunburned bright red. He limps toward us. He is with two boys, each of them maybe ten or eleven years old. I slowly turn back around. The two of us slump down in our chairs in unison. Just trying to make ourselves a little smaller like the Brazilians seated around us.

"We have to do *something*," Nordgren says under his breath.

"We can't stop these people. You heard Costa and Assis. People sacrificed to get us this far, Elder Nordgren. Hopefully not in vain."

"I know."

"We need to think about our families, too," I say.

"Look at what Costa and Assis did," Nordgren says. "They had to pack up their families and run. And we've done nothing but save our precious necks."

"I like my neck," I say. "I like it a lot."

"It is a good neck."

"I'd like to see it on an airplane to somewhere safe anytime now. The same goes for yours, too."

"Just don't move," Nordgren says. "He's going to walk right on by us. That's better either way—being behind him."

We just sit there. We don't talk. We hardly breathe. They walk past us. They hurry like they are late.

"I didn't say anything about stopping the Elbow or Severino, dude. I'm just thinking about them." Nordgren points at the boys' backs as they walk away.

"They look scared."

"We would be too."

"We *would* be? We were. We are."

Nordgren stands up.

I nearly swallow my tongue.

"Relax," he says. "I'm just going to point them out to security. No big deal. They'll never know it was us. You don't even have to come with me."

"Of course I'm going to come with you," I say. "I think it's crazy. I think we should forget about Severino and keep our heads down until this jet shows up. But I'm not letting you out of my sight."

I watch Severino's back as I get up to follow Nordgren. Severino stops short. Turns around. He bends over to pick something up. Maybe his boarding pass. I don't know. He stands up straight again and turns his back to me. I turn my back to him and hurry to catch up with Nordgren. I look again to make sure we are safe. And Severino is standing there looking right at me. His eyes and my eyes meet. He turns again, limping sideways now. He gets out his phone.

"Forget security," I say.

"What?" Nordgren says.

"He sees us! He's making a call!"

We run at him. He doesn't see us coming until the last second. He is focused on his phone. We tackle him to the ground. His phone tumbles across the floor. He fights back harder than I expected. He is strong. Nordgren somehow gets him in a headlock and punches him viciously in the stomach with his free hand. People scream, but they keep their distance.

"He's handicapped," somebody says. "They're beating up a handicapped guy."

"The Americanos just went crazy," somebody else says.

"Handicapped people don't fight like *that*," someone else says.

One of the kids who was with Severino gives Elder Nordgren a kick in the ribs. I look around, but I can't see the other one.

Nordgren rolls over holding his side. That gives me an opening, and I jump on Severino's back. Nordgren gets up, gingerly holding some ribs in place. "Get the police!" he bellows. "Security! Somebody! We need help! This guy is a *kidnapper!*"

Nobody in the crowd seems to move. The circle they have formed around us pulls in tighter, and they can't seem to look away.

"What are you kicking me for?" Nordgren says to the kid. "Why are you helping him? Don't worry, man! We're rescuing you!"

"*Rescuing* me?"

"You don't understand. These people are monsters. Just go, buddy."

The kid comes at Nordgren. He takes a wild swing that Nordgren dodges without really trying. Nordgren easily pushes the kid away.

"I don't want to hurt you," Nordgren says. "I am trying to *help* you. If you don't want help, just get out of the way."

The kid comes at Nordgren again. This time Nordgren punches him hard in the stomach. The kid doubles over, and Nordgren pushes him away. "I'm sorry," he says. "I'm really sorry."

I've got Severino pinned on his face. He still struggles—he is surprisingly strong. All I can do is hold him there. Airport cops finally show up. About five of them—guns drawn—screaming commands. I let go of Severino. Both of us lie exhausted and gasping on the slick tile floor.

Nordgren and I try to explain, but they cuff all of us: Nordgren, me, Severino, and the kid. They walk us back through the terminal toward the security checkpoint and the baggage claim.

I look out the wall of windows, and I see a small jet parked on the tarmac off to one side. A sparkling white Gulfstream that looks decidedly out of place. A Ferrari parked at the end of a long line of flying public buses. There is a guy under the nose of the jet holding a giant wrench. A panel is open, but he is not paying any attention to the guts of plane. He slowly scans the tarmac. He looks expectantly at the terminal. Talks into his collar.

"I didn't do anything wrong," the kid says. "I've got a flight to catch. Please, officer! You've got to let us catch that flight."

"Shut up," Severino says.

"Which flight?" one of the cops says. "Where to?"

"I don't know," the kid says. He looks at the organ trafficker for help. "Miami?"

"Shut up!" Severino says again.

"You don't know?" the cop says. "Or you aren't supposed to say?"

"It doesn't matter," the kid says. "We had a deal. I sold him a kidney, some of my liver, and some bone marrow."

"Is that all?" the cop asks.

"I think so," the kid says.

"Shut up!" Severino says.

"How much?" the cop says.

"Two hundred reais. And—and a free trip too."

Severino just shakes his head in disgust.

"That's illegal," a cop says, clearly proud of himself.

"No, it's not," the kid says.

"Yes, it is," the cop says.

"It's my body, right? My family needs money. So who cares?"

They lock me and Nordgren in a small holding cell. We are in there for a while before another cop comes in. His belly is a mound that hangs down a few inches below his belt. His shirt just barely covers it all.

"Who *are* you guys?" the cop says.

"Have you heard of the Elbow?" I say.

"No," he says.

"Yes," I say. "Yes, you have."

"There isn't a cop in the northeast who hasn't," Nordgren says.

"You attacked a cripple for no apparent reason in the middle of the airport. Not too many style points there, amigos. And yet it didn't seem all that bad when we realized you two are suspected for murder, escaped from prison, and attempting to flee the country."

"That's what we've been trying to tell you," I say. "We aren't criminals. We didn't do anything. I just witnessed a murder."

"Is that right?" The cop gives me a nauseating grin.

"Yes. Some police officers already looked into this. They brought us here, and we just need to catch a flight. We just want to go home. The big guy with the limp—Severino—he works for the Elbow. They are kidnappers. Organ traffickers! You heard that kid. He actually thought he was selling his organs."

"And you doubt that?"

"What? That they're just going to take—what was it?—a kidney, some liver, and some bone marrow too? I doubt that's all they'll take. I doubt he'll ever see any money. I doubt he'll ever see Brazil again."

"Two hundred reais is probably on the low end for all that," the cop says thoughtfully. "I would expect more, personally. The recipient—it obviously depends a lot on the currency and exchange rates—is undoubtedly paying thousands."

"Did they buy that kid a round-trip ticket?" I say. "That might tell you something about what kind of donor they make him out to be."

"Now you're telling me how to do my job?"

I don't respond. I just stare at him, and so does Nordgren. The cop stares back.

"What police officers brought you here?" he finally says. "I need names."

"We can't," I say. "They had to run, too. Because it's the Elbow, right? And they were just two guys. We didn't want to put them in any more danger. They are gone anyway. Far away from here."

"Sure," the cop says.

"Please help us," Nordgren says. "We need to catch a flight. You can save our lives today."

"I'll be back."

He returns about five minutes later. "Back to prison, boys," he says, scratching his mound of stomach. "I'm told you missed an important appointment this morning. The Elbow is sending a car."

"You dirty—" Nordgren shouts.

"You will be happy to know that your pal and his young business associate made their flight on time," he says. "Two hundred reais is a lot of money to a little kid like that. Especially when you consider all the other costs of getting him on the operating table."

"How much did he pay you?"

"Let's go," he says.

"You won't even tell us what our lives were worth to you?"

"No."

"Go to hell."

"I can't give you a number."

"You can't count that high?"

"This might not be a one-off." He grins. "That's the exciting thing. They said they can use a friend inside the airport. Look, I'm not going to ask again. Vamos."

A group of airport cops leads the two of us—our arms still cuffed behind our backs—to a garage. A car pulls in. A large black Mercedes. Private plates, tinted windows, and gold rims with fleur-de-lis emblems on the hubs. Too expensive and garish to be a police vehicle. The airport cops open the back doors on both sides and shove us in. They use the seat belts to strap us down tight. The driver backs out in a hurry. We pull away. The cop who sold us out slowly waves a fat hand in our general direction.

"You two all right?" the driver says.

His voice is unmistakable. "You," I laugh bitterly.

"I tried to warn you," he says.

"Heitor," I say. "You should have just let us disappear."

"Maybe."

We drive north. We come to Boa Viagem, a luxurious beachside Recife neighborhood. On our left, there is a more or less continuous wall of steel and glass and concrete, high-rise apartments. On the right, the sea is green and calm. The white sand slopes gradually away from the highway for two or three hundred yards before meeting the water. Countless bronze bodies—carnaval brings the crowds—walk and sunbathe and play soccer or volleyball on the sand.

"Beautiful," I say under my breath.

"Yeah," Heitor says.

"How far?" Nordgren says.

"From?" Heitor says.

"The prison," Nordgren says.

"Maybe ten kilometers," Heitor says.

"That's where we're going?" I say.

"No," Heitor says.

"The hospital then?" I say.

Heitor doesn't respond. Nordgren and I are both struggling against the cuffs and seat belts. Just looking for any opening, any chance to get away. We see him watching us in the rearview mirror. We ignore him and keep fighting to get loose.

Minutes later, we come up on Boa Vista. Another downtown Recife neighborhood. It is full of high-rise office buildings and apartments and ancient townhouses painted powder blue and violet and teal. The mission office is nearby. There is water everywhere. The ocean, yes, but also a series of green rivers and gray canals crisscrossed by various bridges. Some bridges are large, modern, steel numbers. Others are narrow and cobblestone with barely enough room for one lane of traffic.

"This isn't the way to the hospital," I say.

"How do you know?" Heitor says.

"So you can live with what these people are going to do with us?" Nordgren says. "They are going to cut us open and take what they want and leave us to die."

"We would already be there," Heitor says, "if I were still following the Elbow's orders. I think we should stay to the coast for now. Easier in cities and crowds. Carnaval helps, of course. The crowds."

Nordgren and I look at each other. Heitor checks the rearview mirror. He watches us, apparently looking for a reaction. "You have a better idea?" he says.

"No," I say.

"No," Nordgren agrees.

"We need to ditch the Benz in João Pessoa. Maybe sooner. Attracts too much attention. Probably have to steal something not so well engineered."

"Makes sense," I say.

"This car is one of his favorites," Heitor says.

"His?" I say.

"You know who I mean."

"The Elbow," I say.

"Stealing this car alone is a death sentence."

"Where are you taking us?" Nordgren says.

"Away. Stay to the coast. Keep moving."

"Fair enough," I say.

"That's how far I have thought it out. Eventually you guys make it home. We can drive all the way to Utah if you want to."

"San Diego is far enough," Nordgren says. "You wouldn't like Utah."

"Can we really drive it?" I say.

"The Rodovia Pan-Americana," Heitor says.

"The Pan-American Highway?" I say.

"Yes," he says. "Except for a fifty-mile stretch of rain forest between Panama and Colombia. You ferry around that. Also, you don't go through the Amazon basin. You go around it."

"That should only take a few months," Nordgren says.

"I don't really think driving is the answer," Heitor says. "Too many borders to cross. Maybe you guys catch a flight at some point. Or a boat. Right now we just need to keep moving."

"We should call our presidente," I say. "He can make those kinds of arrangements."

"Sure," Heitor says.

"There was a jet in Recife," Nordgren says. "They sent a private jet for us."

"We can make calls after dark somewhere," Heitor says.

The conversation dies down for a while. Heitor is making good time. We are between Recife and Olinda now, the Atlantic Ocean on our right, the Mata Atlantica—the thin strip of rainforest that runs parallel to the Brazilian coast—on our left. I close my eyes and watch the light on the water flicker through my eyelids. I yawn, deep and slow.

"What about your family?" Nordgren breaks the silence.

"I sent them away. Riberão Preto."

"Is that far enough?" Nordgren says.

"Should be. There are no guarantees."

"You had to tell them, didn't you?" Nordgren says.

"They know."

"How much did you tell them?"

"They know enough," Heitor says ruefully. "Enough to persuade them to suddenly leave everything behind, to get on a bus and never come back. They lost everything—their home, friends, family, the place where they were born and raised."

"How did they take it?"

"I broke their hearts," Heitor says, his voice overcome with emotion. "They are strong people. They will be fine. I sent them with nearly every *centavo* I had saved up. But I could see it in their eyes. I broke their hearts."

"What about the Elbow?" Nordgren says.

"What about him?"

"How does he get away with it?" Nordgren says.

"It won't last. He has so many enemies that prison is the only safe place left. People will learn about the Elbow, and it won't take much. One photo of his cell could blow the lid off the whole thing. His dirty prison guards and cops all hate him. Somebody will get to one of them eventually. And he will land either in the general population or back on the street. He is a dead man either way."

"What about you?" I say.

"I'm going to get you two home."

"Then what?" I say. "Where will you go?"

"Nowhere in particular. Nowhere for very long."

"You are not like them," Nordgren says.

"Them?" Heitor says.

"The Elbow. His men," Nordgren says.

"They are rich and powerful," Heitor says. "They have more guns. They can afford to forget about me, but I'll never pass another day without thinking about them."

"You're not just another traficante," Nordgren says.

"I'm an unemployed traficante," Heitor says. "Worse."

"You are here," I say.

"If you get enough of other people's blood under your fingernails, it doesn't really matter where you are anymore," Heitor says.

"It matters," I say. "I know you don't believe that."

"What am I going to do? Go on a mission?"

"You can still get away from them. You can start over."

"Do you remember our lesson about repentance?" Nordgren says.

"No," Heitor says.

"It is not too late," I say. "That's the gist of it."

"There's no forgiveness for murder. Is there?"

"I don't know," I say. "I believe God can forgive you."

"I think the reach of God's mercy will surprise us all," Nordgren says.

"There is no forgiveness for hurting children," Heitor says. "That's a fact."

"How old were you when you got caught up with the Elbow?" I say.

"Don't make excuses for me."

"You were a child. Weren't you?"

"I was over eight."

"Still," I say.

"We're all children," Nordgren says.

"I will deserve whatever bad things God has in store for me," Heitor says.

"That's the thing about redemption," I say. "You don't deserve it. Nobody does."

A few hours later, we park the Elbow's luxury sedan in front of a supermarket in João Pessoa, another sun-drenched beach town on Brazil's northeastern coast. It is the capital of Paraíba, the state directly north of Pernambuco. Heitor leaves the keys in the ignition and the windows rolled down. "Somebody is going to drive that bad boy far away from our trail before the Elbow ever finds it," he says under his breath as we casually walk away.

Nordgren and I wait in a public park across the street from the beach while Heitor makes alternative travel arrangements. It is shady and cool under vast mango and cashew trees. Heitor pulls up in a bright-green Volkswagen hatchback. It has custom rims and a comically large aftermarket spoiler. I take the front seat. Nordgren jumps in back. We go.

"What, you couldn't find anything more colorful?" I say.

"Four wheels and full tank of gas," Heitor says.

"It sticks out slightly less than the Elbow's boat," Nordgren says. "Right?"

We get back to the highway and drive north. We drive for hours.

We stop that night in Natal, yet another gorgeous beach town, this one two states north of Pernambuco. *Natal* is Portuguese for

"Christmas." Except for skyscrapers off in the distance and white sand dunes here and there, every surface seems to be green and alive. A gentle breeze blows in off the Atlantic. I inhale the salty-sour ocean air with pleasure. We get a room at a cheap motel just off the highway.

Heitor stands lookout while Nordgren and I call Presidente Ford from a pay phone. We assure him that we are safe, and we tell him about Heitor. Presidente Ford tells us to call him back in an hour. When we call back, he tells us we will board the same private jet we saw in Recife at 7:00 a.m. the next morning at a small airport in Caicó. He gives us directions—Caicó is a city in the Sertão, a desert plateau about five hours inland. We try to get a few hours of sleep.

Our drive through the night from the coast to the desert is quiet. We have been jacked up on adrenalin for days, and exhaustion is setting in. "Come with us," I say to Heitor as we pull up to the small airport.

"I can't," Heitor says.

"Why not?" I say.

"I don't have papers. They won't even let me get off the plane. And what if they check my identity? It might get ugly."

"You have a record?"

"I've never been convicted." Heitor kills the ignition. "My picture has been associated with some things. Missing persons cases. Let's go."

We get out of the car. The three of us walk toward the small building we take to be the Caicó airport's terminal. "We'll figure it out," Nordgren says. "Our presidente will help. The church will help. There are politicians and government officials. The church has contacts with people like that. We should at least try."

"What if I bring the danger with me?"

"You won't," Nordgren says.

"I can't put you guys through more of this," Heitor says. "I can't predict how far the Elbow will go to deal with me."

"We should try, Heitor," I say. "You don't have a future here. Do you?"

"Thank you," Heitor says. He stops walking. Nordgren and I pause too. "Thank you. I can't. I just can't. Eventually I'm going south to meet up with my family. To somehow make it up to them."

"You sure?" I say.

"Yes," he says.

"Good-bye, Heitor," I say. I want to reach out and give him a hug. I hold back for some reason. I don't know why.

"Good-bye," Nordgren says.

"Good-bye," Heitor says.

Chapter Twenty-Two

From a distance, Heitor watches Carson and Nordgren climb into the jet. He sits on the hood of the stolen hatchback, which is parked outside the chain-link fence that encircles the Caicó airport's one and only runway. He watches the missionaries fly away. He acts like his eyes are just watering, like they're just irritated by the dust and the dry desert air and the glare of the early morning sun. He blinks them hard and rubs them. He dries them with the bottom of his T-shirt.

Heitor drives into the city and stops at the first neighborhood bakery he sees. He eats his pão doce with pleasure and haste. He looks up. People are watching him. He ignores them. He takes a long drink from his tall glass of passion-fruit juice, tart-sweet and brilliant yellow with tiny bits of black seeds settled on the bottom. A brawny guy in a Brazilian cowboy hat, tooled orange leather with tassels over the ears, comes up to Heitor. "You're not from here," he says.

"Just passing through." Heitor smiles politely. He holds up half a piece of pão doce. "The baker here really knows what he's doing."

The cowboy hat eyes Heitor doubtfully.

"I appreciate the welcome," Heitor says. "This is Caicó, right?"

The cowboy hat moves on, staring Heitor down as he backs away.

Heitor finishes up. He exits the bakery and walks right past the green hatchback. He doesn't even look at it. He walks a few streets further into town and gets directions to the bus station from an old lady perched on a stool in front of a newsstand.

At the station, he buys a one-way ticket on the first bus to Fortaleza, the next big city on the Atlantic coast going north. It is about four-hundred kilometers from Caicó. Heitor sleeps for most of the six-hour-plus bus ride. As the bus pulls into Fortaleza, Heitor gets out his wallet and confirms that the meager sum he started with—he gave his family most of what he'd saved from years of getting his hands dirty for the Elbow—is nearly exhausted.

Heitor spends his first afternoon in Fortaleza and most of the next day looking for work. He winds up on a crew loading and unloading cargo down at the docks. He rents a small room in a neighborhood that, while still on the favela spectrum, could have been much, much worse. Days pass. Heitor works hard, he keeps to himself, and he manages to save a little cash from each paycheck. He plans to head south to find his family once he has enough to buy a cross-country bus ticket.

One night, Heitor can't sleep. For the first time in his life, he gets down on his knees and prays. It is a simple prayer. He tells God that he is sorry. He begs for forgiveness. He prays for his family. And he tells God he will do anything he can to fix what he has done.

The next day before work, Heitor walks down to the edge of the docks. He looks around to make sure nobody is watching. He tosses his gun in the ocean.

Later the same day, Heitor remembers the face of a girl. Her name was Rejane. She was fifteen. The Elbow's operation had kidnapped her. Heitor was ordered to drive Rejane from Olinda to a city hundreds of kilometers inland called Petrolina. There, Heitor was ordered to turn the girl over to a tough guy called Vanderlei. A pimp. A vicious, vile little pimp.

The Elbow sent Heitor because he could pass for Rejane's boyfriend in public if he had to. And because he trusted Heitor implicitly. On that long drive, nearly ten hours on the road, Rejane pleaded endlessly with Heitor to let her go. Attempting to humanize herself to Heitor, she told him about her family. She told him stories from her childhood. She told him about the dreams she had cultivated before being plunged into that nightmare. All those details come back to Heitor now. They overwhelm his mind. He tries, unsuccessfully, to push them back to where they had slumbered harmlessly for so long.

That night, Heitor dreams of Rejane. He sees her again in vivid detail, beautiful and innocent and so afraid. He dreams of her parents, too. He never saw their faces, but he feels their anger and pain and loss, still red hot despite the passage of time. The next day at work, Rejane's face once again occupies Heitor's mind. That night, Rejane and her parents again haunt Heitor's sleep. It is the same thing the next day, too.

The day after that is Sunday. Heitor takes the day off. He finds the address for the nearest Mormon church house. He shows up at seven-thirty even though the earliest services don't start until nine. Heitor waits in the empty chapel. In his eyes, it is eerily similar to the chapel he visited a few times in Olinda. The exact same pulpit. The exact same wood pews. The exact same fluorescent lights and silver-bladed ceiling fans. Even the size and shape of the room seem to be exactly the same. Eventually, a man comes in. He is about thirty-five. Navy-blue suit. Dark, deep-set eyes. He changes some numbers on white cards on a board up at the front.

"Are you a missionary?" Heitor asks.

"I used to be," the man says. "It's been a while."

"Do you have missionaries in this congregation?"

"Yes," the man says, approaching Heitor. "Stick around. I will introduce you." Just like Carson and Nordgren used to do, he offers Heitor his hand. "Bishop Lima," he says. "You are?"

"Silvio," Heitor says. He gives the bishop a firm handshake.

"*Prazer em conhecê-lo,*" Bishop Lima says. A pleasure to know you.

"*Um prazer,*" Heitor says. "You are in charge here?"

"More or less."

"Can I ask you a question?"

"Sure."

"I've been praying for peace of mind pretty much nonstop for days now. I want to know why God won't answer my prayers."

"Something in particular is weighing you down?"

"Yes," Heitor says, his voice trembling with emotion.

"Do you want to talk about it?"

"No. I mean—no."

"Look, God answers prayers. I know that much. Not knowing anything about you, I could only take a wild guess. God gives peace to some. Others he afflicts in a variety of ways. There is mental illness. Guilt. Even the innocent feel sorrow. On and on. I can't help much, you know, unless you give me something to go on."

"I have hurt people. My family. Other people. Let's just leave it at that. I told God I was sorry, and I told him I would do all I could to fix it. Now this. I am miserable. I can't rest. I can't think straight. I can't get these people out of my head. I thought repenting would feel good."

"Have you done what you said?"

"What?"

"Have you done what you can to fix things?"

Heitor furrows his brow. He slowly shakes his head from side to side.

"Maybe that's your answer?" Bishop Lima shrugs. "Maybe not?"

"Yeah," Heitor says. "I don't know."

"Like I said, Silvio, stick around. We've been known to dispense some peace to the weary-hearted every now and then. That's the idea, anyway."

"I will," Heitor says.

"And if you want to talk sometime, really talk, I will be here."

"Sure. Thanks."

"I've got to run," the bishop says, checking his watch. "I'll be back. Meetings start soon."

"*Até logo,*" Heitor says.

"*Até.*"

Bishop Lima leaves in a hurry. Heitor waits for a minute. Then he gets up and goes. He walks back to his rented room. He empties his savings, a jar of real notes, out on the bed. He counts them and straightens them out and stuffs them in his wallet. He walks to the central bus terminal and buys a ticket on the next bus to Recife.

Heitor doesn't make it to Recife until well after dark. Instead of spending the rest of his savings on a hotel room, he catches a bus from the terminal to the nearest beach, Boa Viagem. He sits under a palm tree and watches the waves crash on the sand. He watches lovers holding hands as they walk up and down the beach, their bare feet coated in fine sand or bathed in the gentle surf. He sits there for hours, just watching, before finally falling asleep.

Heitor feels a sudden chill. He wakes up to a glorious golden sunrise over the Atlantic. It makes him feel wonder that he hasn't felt since he was a small child. It makes him think about his family. He imagines them in the south. He wonders if his little sisters have grown, changed. The thought of them pulls his mind back to Rejane.

He gets up. He stretches and brushes sand off his pants. He catches a bus to Olinda. He knows roughly where to go; he hasn't forgotten the home Rejane described to him. He gets off the bus and climbs the hill in the ancient part of town. Near the top, he turns down a narrow lane. People are out here and there sweeping their porches or hanging laundry to dry or sipping coffee over newspapers. One by one, Heitor asks them if they knew Rejane. He asks if they know her parents. Most make like they can't understand one word of what he is saying. They stare for a minute and then go on with whatever they were doing. Or they give him a deeply troubled look that seems to mean *People don't just say that name around here. Especially strangers.*

Eventually, a woman in a bathrobe beating a rug with a broom tells Heitor she knows the family. She leads him to a house on the next street. She opens the front door and asks Heitor to follow her inside. She shows him a couch and asks him to sit.

"What do you want?" she says, standing above him.

"I need to talk to Rejane's parents," Heitor says.

"About what?"

"Rejane."

"Don't screw with these people. I'm Rejane's aunt. Trust me, they can't take anything funny right now. And there's nothing here for you to gain. Understand?"

"I just need a minute. I don't hope to gain anything. I will say my piece and leave."

She glares at Heitor. She gives him a shrug, sorrowful and resigned. "Lucas," she calls into the house, "Isaura. You have a guest."

"Who?" a woman calls back.

"A young man. It's about Rejane." She says *Rejane* softly, tentatively, as if forming that sound with her lips causes her and others exquisite pain.

Lucas and Isaura, Rejane's parents, appear after a minute. They do not sit. Their faces are drawn.

"I have information about your daughter," Heitor says.

"Who are you?" Lucas says.

"My name isn't important," Heitor says. "I'm a former gangster. I may know where she is."

"You think she is alive?" he says.

"I hope so."

"Go on."

Heitor tells them about Petrolina and the pimp called Vanderlei. Both parents' emotions boil to the surface. They sob violently but without much sound. Heitor waits for them. As they regain control, he describes the location of Vanderlei's brothel. He hands Lucas a rudimentary map drawn on a scrap of newsprint. "You can bring her home," Heitor says.

"Thank you," the father says through bitter tears.

"No," Heitor says. "If you only knew. Don't thank me. I'm sorry. Like I said, I used to—I helped them—the people who took her. I am so sorry."

"I understand," the father says.

"Please, just don't tell anyone I was here."

"All right."

Heitor leaves, apologizing once more. He walks quickly down the street. His objective accomplished, he lets himself think about the fact that Olinda is crawling with the Elbow's men, a large network of violent scum, all of whom know his face. Something else weighs heavily on Heitor's mind: he is nearly out of money again. He certainly doesn't have enough for a bus ticket back to Forteleza or some other equally distant city.

He keeps walking. He decides to walk all the way to his parents' house. Going there is risky, but it's better than the alternatives. He hopes to find something, anything, that will help him leave Olinda today and never come back. His family took off in a hurry, and they could have left things behind that he could pawn or sell. He fears the house will be occupied by squatters. Or ransacked and empty. Heitor moves fast, and he keeps his eyes open for trouble. For the first time since he dumped it in the ocean, Heitor truly misses his gun.

The house looks the same from a distance. He starts to jog. He quickly climbs over the perimeter wall and walks around back. He is amazed to see his motorcycle parked on the back patio, exactly where he left it. Apparently the Elbow's men didn't bother to come get it, and the small-time criminals around the neighborhood knew better than to mess with Heitor.

He kicks in the back door of the house and quickly looks things over. There's no money in any of the usual hiding places. The valuables, jewelry and the like, are all gone. What's left, Heitor decides, would be too much hassle to deal with on the back of a motorcycle. He grabs an atlas of Brazil to help him navigate the long ride south. He rolls it up and stuffs it in his pocket. He smashes the glass out of the family portrait hanging over the sofa, tears the picture out of the frame, folds it several times, and stuffs it in his other pocket.

Heitor goes back to the motorcycle. He checks the gas tank. Nothing but fumes. Maybe enough to get to the nearest gas station. He pushes it around front. He curses, suddenly remembering the lock on the front gate. He runs around back again, goes inside the house through the back door, and grabs the spare key. He gets the gate open and pushes the motorcycle out into the street. He kick-starts it and speeds off, leaving the front gate gaping wide open.

The motorcycle sputters and dies a few blocks short of the gas station. Heitor jumps off and pushes it the rest of the way. He is standing at the pump unscrewing the chrome lid of the tank when he hears the gunshots. A series of loud cracks, an extremely familiar sound to Heitor. *Semi-automatics,* he tells himself. *Two of them. They are close.*

People on the street scream and run and take cover. Heitor tumbles forward over the motorcycle as countless bullets penetrate his shoulders and back. He slides off the motorcycle—he hits the ground face down. He feels no pain at first. It comes over him in waves. A series of increasingly intense burning sensations in his neck, shoulders, lungs, and left hip. He watches his blood pour out onto the petroleum-stained concrete.

He tries to get up. He can't. He tries to roll over and only makes it halfway. He gasps for air. He digs in his pocket and pulls out the family portrait, but he can't get it unfolded. The right side of his body has gone limp. He clutches the folded portrait tightly in his left hand.

Heitor looks up at the sky, blue and clear. *This is it,* he tells himself. He hears something that pulls him back to earth. The sound of tires squealing on asphalt. He looks. A car circles around and stops in the street in front of the gas station. The driver's door swings open. Heitor gasps for air as he watches. Severino gets out of the car and limps toward him.

"It *is* you." Severino laughs. "I couldn't believe my ears when I got the call. You had everything, Heitor. Money. Power. Women. He loved you more than he loved his own son! He held nothing back from you. And you—you threw it all away. And for what? Your family? A couple of religious freaks? I mean, it's embarrassing."

Severino takes hold of the gas-pump nozzle. He slowly lifts it out of its holder. He squeezes the handle, spraying gasoline all over Heitor. Iridescent swirls of fuel catch the sunlight here and there on the growing pool of red under Heitor. Severino steps back awkwardly, strikes a match, and tosses it in Heitor's direction. A burst of flame forces Severino backward—he stumbles and falls. Gracelessly, he gets back on his feet. "You will be famous," he says, pulling out his phone. He casually shoots some video. He zooms in on Heitor, writhing in pain, still gasping for air. "This is what it looks like, amigo. You don't cross the Elbow."

Chapter Twenty-Three

"He's dead," says Alberto's voice through the phone speaker. "Those bastards killed my son."

I look at Nordgren. I watch that hit him. He winces. Shuts his eyes and rubs them. Goes to say something, but nothing comes out.

"Heitor is dead," I softly say to Lilly, who doesn't speak Portuguese. She is standing by my side; her arm suddenly reaches around me. It pulls vice-tight around my back like she's trying to brace me from the shock of Alberto's call.

"Hello?" says Alberto. "Did I lose you?"

"We're here," Nordgren says. "We're just—we're speechless."

• • •

Months have passed since Nordgren and I came home from Brazil. We hadn't seen each other since the day the jet landed in

Salt Lake City. Lilly, my fiancée now, and I flew into San Diego last night. She insisted on meeting Nordgren, and not just in the reception line after our wedding.

We stayed up late last night catching up; the conversation probably bored Lilly out of her mind. It turns out that both Nordgren and I gave typical homecoming talks in which we didn't mention, even obliquely, the circumstances under which we left Brazil. Also, both of us have been subjected to a series of meetings with general authorities and church missionary department employees to go over what happened in excruciating detail. Both of us have been told that our story does not constitute a faith-promoting experience. Both of us were repeatedly encouraged to never speak of it publicly.

Both of us watched and read the news stories with interest. They were vague when they were not completely inaccurate. They displayed grainy pictures of us and said that we had witnessed a crime. They reported that we had cooperated fully with the local authorities in their investigation. They claimed that we had been kept in a safe place for a few days until we could safely leave the country and fly home to our families. Neither of us did interviews, and the church didn't comment publicly except to say that we were safe at home, that we had been honorably released, and that our requests to serve out the final months of our two-year commitments someplace else had been respectfully declined.

The three of us were on our way out the door to pick up Nordgren's date and head to the beach when the phone rang.

"It's for you," Nordgren's mom said to him. "Collect call from Brazil."

"This ought to be good," Nordgren said dryly. "Probably the Elbow." We went back inside. Nordgren took the receiver and accepted the call. He put Alberto on speaker, who promptly told us about Heitor.

...

"Is it safe for you to be calling?" Nordgren says.
"I think so. I'm on a pay phone. Not very traceable."
"We're sorry for your loss," I say.
"Are you all right?" Nordgren says.
"We're still here," Alberto says.
"How did it happen?" I say.
"We hadn't seen him for weeks, of course. We found out about everything. He sent us away. We didn't know when we would see him. We had no contact. We just hoped and prayed. We told one person in Olinda where we were going. So we get a call from her. She says to me, 'They shot Heitor, and they burned his body, and I thought you should know.'"
"I'm sorry, Alberto," Nordgren says.
"That's awful," I say.
"I just had to tell someone who would understand," Alberto says. "Here, we don't use our real names. We don't tell people we are from Olinda. In our new life, we never even had a son."
"Where was he when it happened?" I say.
"He was in Olinda. Near our home. Gassing up his motorcycle."

"Why did he go back?" I say.

"We don't know. We can't make any sense out of it."

"I can't help feeling responsible," I say.

"Don't say that," Alberto says. "Heitor was in so much trouble. I shudder to think about all the evil he did in his short life. It's not your fault, Elder Carson. You outlived my son for more than one reason."

"He saved our lives," I say. "He's the main reason we survived. We were dead men walking, and he came back for us."

"Alberto," Nordgren says. "Heitor was sorry. You should know that. He repented. I believe you will see him again."

"If I do," Alberto says, "it will be thanks to you guys."

"We can't take any credit," Nordgren says.

"You can," Alberto says. "You should."

"How's your family?" Nordgren says.

"Like I said, we are still here. If the sun comes up again tomorrow, I suppose we will get up too. What else can we do?"

There is a long pause.

"How did you get Elder Nordgren's number?" I say. I can't help thinking about whether other Brazilians have tried to locate us. About how easy it would be.

"He wrote it in the Book of Mormon you guys gave Heitor. Under the number, it says *You will always have a place to crash in California.*"

"We love you," Nordgren says. "Again, we are very sorry about your loss."

"Send our love to your family," I say. "Take care of them."

"I will."

"We should—" I was about to say *visit sometime*, but I realize that neither Nordgren nor I will ever return to Brazil.

"We probably shouldn't have much contact after this," Alberto says. "To be safe."

"You're probably right," Nordgren says.

We say our good-byes. We wait for Alberto to hang up. We can hear him on the other end waiting for us to do the same thing. Finally, the line goes dead.

www.ingramcontent.com/pod-product-compliance
Ingram Content Group UK Ltd.
Pitfield, Milton Keynes, MK11 3LW, UK
UKHW041417180426
11947UKWH00007B/175